SEA FOG

SEA FOG

A Folly Beach Halloween Mystery

BILL NOEL
ANGELICA CRUZ

Other Folly Beach Mysteries by Bill Noel

Folly

The Pier

Washout

The Edge

The Marsh

Ghosts

Missing

Final Cut

First Light

Boneyard Beach

Silent Night

Dead Center

Discord

A Folly Beach Mystery COLLECTION

Dark Horse

Joy

A Folly Beach Mystery COLLECTION II

No Joke

Relic

A Folly Beach Mystery COLLECTION III

Faith

A Folly Beach Christmas Mystery COLLECTION

Tipping Point

Front cover photo and design by Bill Noel

Author photos by Susan Noel

ISBN: 978-1-948374-51-4

Enigma House Press

Goshen, Kentucky 40026

www.enigmahousepress.com

Chapter One

The last time I visited a Halloween haunted house I was thirteen, maybe fourteen. It's hard to remember exactly how old since it was more than fifty-five years ago. What I do remember was the female classmate I went with screaming from the spider-webbed entry until we exited the darkened house between two skeletons grabbing at our arms. True, there were scary scenes in the house, but to impress the girl squeezing my arm enough to cut off circulation, I acted like I regularly sauntered through dark corridors with axes swinging overhead and ghosts waving their translucent hands in my face. The other thing I remember was that she refused to have anything to do with me the remainder of the school year as if I was responsible for her traumatic adventure. I would've been wiser convincing dad to drop us off at the ice-cream shop rather than the haunted house. Live and learn.

Fast forward a few decades, when my best friend Charles Fowler called to suggest it'd be fun if we relived some of our youth and attended a haunted house being staged in a large, white frame house adjacent to Loggerhead's Restaurant. I said no, perhaps louder than a simple no, then reminded him we didn't know any young people we could escort through the exhibit.

He said, "What's that have to do with anything?"

"Nothing other than we're old enough to be mistaken for mummies."

Charles laughed. "Speak for yourself. I was talking to a couple of guys at Planet Follywood last night. They said they went through it and had a good time. Said there were a bunch of older people doing the same thing."

"Older people?"

"Yeah. Some were in their thirties."

"You do know that's less than half our ages."

Charles is two years younger than me.

"Picky, picky, picky. So, what time you meeting me there?"

Arguing with Charles was like arguing with a rabid raccoon, so I said six-thirty, hoping it was before the crowd arrived.

Being Thursday, I figured attendance at Folly Beach's answer to Lizzie Borden's House would be light with fewer people around to laugh at us for taking in the attraction, so I waited for him in Loggerhead's parking lot forty-five minutes before the time we agreed to meet. For those who might not know Charles, thirty minutes early was his definition of being on time and it was easier to adjust to his idiosyncrasy than to convert him to reality.

Ten minutes later, he skidded around the corner on his classic Schwinn bicycle, nearly colliding with a Ford pickup truck travelling the correct direction on the one-way street. Charles was breathing heavily as he parked his bike while looking at his bare wrist where normal people wore a watch, his way of indicating he was on time. Years ago, he'd confided to owning a watch, but I'd never seen it.

"Whew," he said as he took a deep breath. "Almost late. Know why I'm wearing this?" He pointed to his gray, long-sleeve sweatshirt with Michigan State in green letters on the front.

"You're cold?" I said, knowing it wasn't the answer he was fishing for.

He shook his head; a motion people often resort to after listening to Charles for a period. "No, silly boy, they offer a course called 'Surviving the Coming Zombie Apocalypse.'"

"You know that how, more importantly, why?"

"Ghost-hunter Google told me. Figured it's appropriate for our adventure through the haunted house."

"Oh," I said, often a reaction to his insightful comments.

"Knew you'd be impressed. Ready to get the heebie-jeebies scared out of us?"

I didn't get a chance to say no since he left his bike leaning against the wooden bench facing the street and headed toward the large tent erected in the attraction's side yard. A large white sign with ENTER AT YOUR OWN RISK painted in blood-red block letters was taped above the tent's open flap.

It was a half hour before sunset but the strobe lights on each side of the tent's entry bounced orange, and black ghost-shaped images off the tent's sides. A half-dozen high-school-aged teens were lined in front of a table where a man dressed like a farmer wearing bib overalls was selling admission tickets. I didn't know whether to laugh or roll my eyes at the faux arrow sticking out of his head. So far, to my relief, no one recognized me. That was until someone tapped me on the shoulder.

"Well if it isn't my good buddy, Chris Landrum," Stanley Kremitz said as he put his arm around my shoulder. "You're a sight for sore eyes."

Charles said he'd get our tickets. I chalked it up as his wanting to avoid Stanley rather than being overcome with generosity, a rare occurrence.

Stanley was an acquaintance I'd run into several times a year ago when he provided information and was for a time a suspect, in a murder I'd become more involved in than I wanted to be. He was a nice, friendly man but had never met a cliché he didn't like, and repeat.

He wore black slacks, a black sweatshirt with a skeleton on the front, and a ballcap with *Staff* on the crown.

"Working the haunted house?" I asked. A safe guess considering his attire.

"A win-win, my friend. I enjoy getting out of the house and feel like I'm helping the wonderful charity benefitting from this shindig." He chuckled. "Besides, Veronica says me doing stuff like this helps keep her sane. Out of sight, out of mind, you know."

Veronica was Stanley's wife, or his better half in Stanley-speak. I understood what she meant about him not being home.

"Oh."

Stanley looked around like he just noticed me standing by myself. "You taking a youngster through?"

Yes, it's Charles, but I didn't share that with Stanley.

"No. How're ticket sales?" I said to avoid the next logical question he might ask.

"Selling like hotcakes."

"Good to hear it."

I looked around to find Charles and a possible rescue. He was at the side of the elevated house avoiding eye contact with Stanley.

"Better get in, Stanley. Good seeing you."

He smiled. "Good luck in there. Not everybody gets out alive, you know. You can take that to the bank."

I would rather face a house full of ghosts, goblins, serial killers, and a psychopath or two than spend more time with the cliché king.

"Thanks for that information."

It wasn't hard to figure out where we were to go next. A four-by-eight-foot sheet of plywood was painted white and attached over a window on the side of the house. The structure was less than a block from the ocean, so I suspected during hurricane season, the wood was used to protect the window from storm damage. COFFIN ISLAND HAUNTED HOUSE was written on the plywood in red paint which ran down each letter looking like blood or simply a poor paint job. During its early history, Folly was dubbed Coffin Island.

I joined Charles where a staff member at the bottom of the steps stamped our hands with the image of something that looked like a spider. We headed up the steps. Metal arches were over three of the stairs with artificial spider webs draping down enough to brush against our heads. If it were darker, visitors would get an eerie feeling with the webs touching them.

"What were you and Stanley shooting the breeze about?" Charles laughed at his use of a cliché.

"Funny."

A man on the landing at the top of the stairs emoted screeching sounds as he waved his arm toward the door. I didn't speak screech, so I didn't know what he was saying, but his motions indicated he wanted our tickets and waved us into the pitch-black hallway. The non-profit organization sponsoring the event must've gotten a good price on strobe lights. Everywhere I turned, the flashing, distracting lights disoriented me, achieving their intended goal.

The amplified sound of rattling chains drew our attention to a door leading to a large room where a coffin was lightly illuminated in the corner. I heard screams coming from a couple of the teens who preceded us into the house. I hadn't seen anything to get that level of fear but wouldn't be surprised if something terrifying was coming around the next corner or two.

Before I gave more thought to what was coming next, someone dressed like a mummy slipped up beside me. No, I didn't scream, but will admit to coming close. The creature, man, woman, whatever put its arm around mine and led me to the coffin. Out of the corner of my eye, I saw Charles following at a safe distance.

Fake fog began to fill the area around the coffin and the mummy nudged me closer to the prop—what I assumed to be a prop. Sinister laughter coming from several different voices reverberated off the walls.

The top of the coffin suddenly flipped open and someone dressed like Chucky sat up wielding a knife. I'd never seen the Chucky movies about a serial killer and voodoo practitioner who, after being shot, somehow became a child-sized doll, but did have to take a giant step back after spotting the lethal weapon. Okay, yes, I'm a coward, but, hey, who wouldn't be faced with someone sitting up and staring at you from inside a coffin. Charles's laugh was louder than those coming from the sound system. I didn't want to go Chucky on him, but revenge wasn't far from my mind.

The top of the coffin closed as quickly as it had opened. A howling sound pierced the air and a spotlight's beam penetrated the artificial fog as it reappeared in the room. The light shone on a door at the side of the room revealing a sign reading *Blackbeard's Bedroom*. The tour-guide mummy waved us to the door then stepped aside as the door slowly creaked open. There were no strobe lights, fake fog, or strange creatures within sight. This time, Charles took the lead and stuck his head in the door and looked around. I figured the mummy hadn't led us to an empty room, so I stood behind Charles to wait for the next fright. After all, Blackbeard's bedroom wasn't designed to give visitors a warm, fuzzy feeling. Edward Teach, aka Blackbeard, the scary pirate from the early 1700s had once resided on Folly and was known for putting smoking fuses in his long, stringy black hair to frighten his victims.

Folly's Blackbeard incarnation wasn't quite that frightening, but when he put his hand on Charles's shoulder, my friend jumped higher than I'd ever seen him levitate. I didn't laugh, but came close, as Charles quickly backed out of the room.

The mummy then nudged us into what was the kitchen although there were no appliances, and only one of the cabinets had been installed. Before I looked around to see what frightful site we were supposed to see, someone screamed. It was loud, scary, and not recorded.

Instead of hearing recorded laughter or other sound associated with a haunted house, someone on the far side of the kitchen yelled, “Get the lights!”

Overhead lights came on temporarily blinding me. The door leading from the kitchen to the back porch swung open and two men wearing the same kind of black sweatshirts and hats Stanley had worn rushed into the room, looked at Charles and me, then headed into a large, walk-in pantry where two teens were backed against the shelves. One of the teenagers had his hands over his face, the other pointing to something on the floor.

Charles and my visit to Folly’s haunted house quickly became a nightmare as we stepped in the pantry and stared at a body on the floor.

Chapter Two

The phrase *running around like chickens with their heads cut off* came to mind as a staff member yelled for everyone to leave the house. He didn't have to say it twice to the two teens who were out the back door as quickly as a cheetah. The older man waved for Charles and me to leave, then stared at the body before rushing out to start herding those who followed us into the house to the exit. The other man held his hand over his mouth. I was afraid he was going to lose his latest meal. He took two deep breaths, appeared to regain composure before glancing in each corner of the pantry like he was afraid someone wielding a knife would jump out at him, then rushed out of the room.

Despite being told to leave, Charles motioned me closer to the body and knelt near the unmoving person.

"Know who he is?" Charles said as he looked up at me.

The man's head was turned at an odd angle, so I couldn't get a clear look at his face. He was in his forties, white with light-brown hair, and wearing jeans with raveled cuffs and a black, long-sleeve sweatshirt. He didn't appear to be one of the actors in the house but could've had a behind-the-scenes role.

"Don't think so. You?"

The recorded music and haunting sound effects came to a screeching halt and were replaced by the sound of sirens from Folly's police and fire vehicles approaching the house.

The gruff voice of the older of the two staff members barked, "I told you to leave."

"On our way," Charles said although he was still bent over the body.

"Now!"

Before the man physically evicted us, Officer Trula Bishop barged into the room. I'd known Trula for four years since she began working as a Public Safety Officer in Folly's Department of Public Safety, more commonly known as a cop in the police department. She was professional, competent, and someone I'd trust in the most difficult situation.

She glanced at Charles and me, nodded at the worker, before walking over to the corpse, bending to get a better look at his face, then saying, "Anyone know who he is?"

Instead of answering her question, the staff member again told Charles and me to leave.

"Sir," Bishop said, "I'm speaking to these gentlemen as well as to you."

I was glad Charles didn't stick his tongue out at the bossy staff member.

I said, "Officer Bishop, I don't recall seeing him before tonight."

"Me either," Charles added, not to be left out.

Two firefighters who double as EMTs entered the room

and immediately went to the body, ignoring Officer Bishop and the rest of us.

Bishop glared at the staff member. "Sir, what's your name?"

"Lester, ma'am. Lester Holmes."

Bishop jotted it down in a small notebook she pulled out of her pocket. "Mr. Holmes, do you know who this is?" She pointed to the body like he wouldn't have known who she was referring to.

"Umm, no officer."

Bishop looked back at the body and then at Lester. "He didn't work in the haunted house?"

"I don't believe so."

"You're not sure?"

"Not really, ma'am. There are a lot of people involved in the project. Actors dressed like ghosts, skeletons, Blackbeard, serial killers; then the technical crew running the lights, sound, fog machine, and other special effects. I don't see everyone. My job is to make sure once guests finish the tour, they leave down the back stairs."

"You don't see everyone working here?"

"No. I don't get here until right before we open. Leave as soon as the last guest is out the door."

"Okay, Mr. Holmes, please go out the back door and wait at the bottom of the stairs. A detective will want to talk with you once he arrives."

Folly is in Charleston County, South Carolina, a stone's throw from beautiful and historic Charleston. Its small police force isn't large enough or trained to handle murder investigations on the island so that's delegated to the Charleston County Sheriff's Office.

Lester started to say something, but apparently thought

better of it, before saying, "Yes ma'am." He gave a tentative salute to Officer Bishop and back peddled out of the room.

Bishop rolled her eyes as he left, then turned to Charles and me. "Okay, Mr. Chris, Mr. Charles, what do you two know about what happened?"

"Trula, I'm afraid not much. Charles and I were going through the exhibit when someone, probably one of the teenagers who went through ahead of us, started screaming. We came in here, saw the two teens and the body. Charles, anything to add?"

"That's about it, Trula," Charles said, one of the few times he was at a loss of words.

"Then I've got another question," Bishop said, "Why in holy hell were you two alleged adults, senior-citizen adults, walking through a haunted house?"

Excellent question, I thought. I turned to the instigator of our visit to respond.

"Thought it'd be fun to see what scares kids nowadays," Charles said, then smiled.

This time Trula didn't hide rolling her eyes in front of the intended recipients.

One of the EMTs moved beside Bishop before she could humiliate us more. He cleared his throat to get her attention, then said, "Officer Bishop, he's deceased."

I was surprised when she didn't roll her eyes at his massive understatement.

"Call the coroner's office. I'll call the Chief and the Sheriff's Office." She turned to Charles and me. "Guys, sure you don't know anything else about what happened?"

I assured her we didn't.

"Then head out the back door and join the others who were here. Don't leave the property."

It would've taken a tsunami to get Charles to leave before learning more about what had happened.

We walked down the back stairs where a cluster of people was herded off to the side by a couple of police officers. We reached the bottom of the steps and were directed to the gathered group by an officer I didn't know.

The group was interesting to say the least. The mummy, Chucky from the coffin, Blackbeard, and two other actors dressed like witches I hadn't remembered seeing in the house were clustered together. It was just after sunset, so they didn't look as scary as they had in the dark, fog-filled house. Two men in their twenties and one slightly younger woman were dressed in all black including caps that looked appropriate for bank robbers were near the scary actors. I assumed they were the special effects team. Two other casually dressed men were standing near the actors and staff.

Standing a few feet apart from the cast and crew, I recognized the two teens who'd been in front of us, and six others, four teens and two youngsters roughly ten years old, were huddled together.

Fortunately, the temperature was mild for late October and while a couple of those gathered were shivering, it wasn't because of the weather. A police officer I did recognize was interviewing two of the teens and taking notes. Officer Allen Spencer had been new to the force when I moved to Folly nearly a dozen years ago. He and I'd talked countless times since then.

Allen noticed Charles and me as we joined the group, gave a doubletake, and looked to see who was with us.

He finished his interview with one of the teens and came our way.

"Chris, Charles, you playing fossils in the house or taking youngsters through?"

"Funny, Officer Spencer," I said.

Charles said, "I'm the youngster Chris was escorting."

Allen smiled. "Charles, I didn't mean mental age."

"Funny, Officer Spencer," Charles said.

Spencer looked around to see if anyone was listening. Seeing no one, he said, "Just kidding, Charles. What happened? I got stuck out here and have no idea what's going on. That is, except for the contradictory stories I'm hearing from the folks who were in there."

"Allen, I'm afraid we can't add much." I shared what little we knew, then asked if anyone he had interviewed knew the identity of the victim.

"No one claimed to have seen him before, but only the two teenagers over there saw the body." He pointed to the two who had been in front of us in the house.

Charles rubbed his chin. "You're telling us no one in that group even saw the body?"

"Correct. The staff member said the pantry where the body's located isn't part of the exhibit, or whatever you'd call the haunted house parts of the house. The two who found it didn't wait for the mummy tour guide and rushed ahead and opened a door they weren't supposed to open. The staff member said it should've been locked. The kids said it wasn't. They figured they were supposed to open it and be scared by something. Don't think they thought it'd be a real horror.

Add Charles and me to that group.

Chapter Three

"What are you two troublemakers doing going through a haunted—oh crap, never mind," Chief Cindy LaMond said through gritted teeth as she pulled us out of the group like a sheepdog herding two recalcitrant sheep out of the herd and escorted us to a detached garage in the rear of the property.

I'd known Chief LaMond since my second year on Folly and considered she and her husband Larry good friends.

"Chief," Charles said as Cindy opened the garage door and shooed us in, "I thought Chris would like to see how great a job some of your local folks did providing a wonderful adventure for your younger citizens this Halloween season."

Cindy closed the door after we were in the garage. "Charles, I'm from East Tennessee; grew up around farm animals of all kinds; shoveled you-know-what until my arms felt like they were falling off and my nose screamed for an air freshener."

Charles nodded. "So?"

"Glad you asked. I went into law enforcement to escape that. Then lo and behold, here I am with you spreading more crap than I ever ran across in the barnyard. Since I'm Chief and know everything, you dragged the old guy you're with through the house to be nosy, which happens to be your biggest vice, and something you do better than anyone I've ever known. How am I doing?"

"Chief, Abraham Lincoln said, 'It has been my experience that folks who have no vices have very few virtues.'"

"Cindy LaMond said you just added another clump of crap to the pile."

Enough, I thought but didn't say or quote anyone saying it. "Chief, is there a reason we're here instead of out there with the others?"

"Yes. I don't know many of the folks from the house we've corralled, and the three I know, aren't known for reliability. Despite the pain in my rear you two cause, you're reliable and observant."

"You're a wise lady," Charles said.

"Don't forget the part about you being a pain in my posterior."

Over the years, Charles and I had stumbled upon a few murders and despite not having law enforcement training or experience, had managed to help the police bring some killers to justice. In fact, Charles is a self-proclaimed private detective. In the process, we'd inadvertently interfered with police investigations, incurred the wrath of numerous law enforcement officials, including Chief LaMond, and had come close to being killed on more than one occasion. Despite that, Cindy had learned to trust our, or at least my, judgement and had even sought our help. She would deny it regardless of the kind of oath she would be put under. I didn't blame her. I often questioned my judgment and that of Charles and a few of our friends who've gotten into things we shouldn't have.

"Chief," I said, "what do you want to know?"

"Your version of what you saw, experienced, and your gut reactions about what went on in there." She nodded the direction of the house.

We alternated telling her everything beginning with arriving at the tent then ending when Officer Bishop arrived. The Chief asked if we saw anything unusual during our time in the house.

Charles smiled. "Anything unusual?" He rubbed his chin. "You mean other than a mummy grabbing my arm, a clown sitting up in a coffin waving a knife in Chris's face, and, oh yeah, Blackbeard scaring the, well, stuff out of me?"

"Let me rephrase, anything other than what you'd expect to find in a Halloween haunted house?"

"Not really," I said. "It was early, so I doubt many people had been through before us. The only two I saw ahead of us were the two teenagers, the ones who found the body."

Cindy shook her head. "That's all?"

Charles said, "Afraid so, Chief."

I nodded.

"Crap."

"Chief," I said, "let me ask you something."

"Could I stop you? Never mind, go ahead."

"Who owns the house?"

She removed a small notebook from her pocket. It was like the ones Officers Bishop and Spencer were using.

"Fred Robinson. He's new to the area; bought it a few months ago."

Charles said, "Who's he?"

"Don't know much. He's a dentist with an office on James Island; think it's one of several offices in a practice out of Savannah. I talked to him once. Jotted his name down since he was new here. He was meeting with his contractor in the front yard. Said he was fixing the house up. Not sure if he planned to live in it or use it as a rental. He didn't offer additional information. Not a very friendly fellow. Why?"

"Curious," I said. "Wondering if the body could've had something to do with the owner."

Officer Bishop stuck her head in the door. "Chief, Detective Adair's here."

I'd met Kenneth Adair with the County Sheriff's Office three years ago when he was lead detective on the murder of a college student. He'd focused on a friend of mine as the prime suspect. Detective Adair and I weren't on the friendliest terms since I nosed into the investigation and helped prove my friend innocent. It mattered little to him that I also helped catch the murderer. Go figure.

Cindy said, "I'll be right there."

Bishop left to relay the message, and Cindy said, "Guys, let me know if you learn anything that may be helpful." Before she left, she added, "Now get your butts back out there and stay with the group from in the house until Adair talks to you."

Charles turned to me after Cindy had left. "Chris, you hear that?"

"What?"

"She wants us to find out who killed the guy."

That wasn't my interpretation, not by a long shot.

That'd never stopped Charles. I had a hunch this time would be no different.

We returned to the group still huddled near the steps leading from the house. Officer Spencer was talking to one of the teenage girls while another officer I didn't know was in deep conversation with one of the witches. We received a couple of curious stares from others in the group, most likely because we'd been singled out by Chief LaMond. Someone had distributed bottles of water to the assembled group and two of the crew members were off to the side puffing on cigarettes.

Chief LaMond was near the tent at the front of the property talking with Detective Adair. The detective was in his late thirties, roughly six-foot-one, thin, and sporting a buzz cut. He wore a white shirt, navy blazer, slacks with a sharp crease, and highly polished wingtips. He looked like he could've come from a corporate board meeting, although I doubted it since he was dressed like he'd been each time I'd seen him during our previous encounters.

Adair and the Chief finished their conversation and approached. He whispered something to Cindy, then turned to the group.

"Ladies and gentlemen, I'm Detective Adair from the County Sheriff's Office. I apologize for you having to be here so long and know this has been a trying evening. Chief LaMond and I will be talking to each of you one-on-one over by the garage. I know you want to get out of here, so we'll be as quick as possible. I'll be back momentarily."

He and Cindy went up the back stairs and entered the house.

It was well after dark and Charles and I were the last to

be interviewed, so I learned *as quick as possible* was two hours, twenty minutes. I apparently drew the short straw and had the privilege of being interviewed by Adair; Charles lucked out with Chief LaMond. We were a few minutes into the interview before Adair remembered me from previous encounters. From his body language and sighs during some of my responses, his recollections weren't any more positive than mine. Once he figured he couldn't learn anything significant from me, he gave me his card, told me to call if I remembered anything else, then said I could leave. He didn't say anything about me not nosing around. I didn't know it for a fact but would put money on Chief LaMond telling Charles not to.

Charles headed for his bike; I started home when I noticed a crowd of onlookers standing on the sidewalk across the street from the house. The group was in front of the Charleston Oceanfront Villas, an expansive, four-story, oceanfront condo complex. Police and fire activity are a spectator sport on Folly, drawing crowds of locals and visitors. It was dark so I couldn't get a good look at the faces, but thought I recognized Preacher Burl Costello as he was illuminated by the red and blue strobes from two emergency vehicles. I'd met Burl a few years ago when he arrived on Folly and founded First Light, a nondenominational church that meets most Sundays on the beach. With his five-foot-five-inch height, portly body, milk-chocolate colored mustache, and balding head, he would've been hard to miss.

The preacher was standing with his arm around the shoulders of a young lady, around ten years old, although I'm terrible at guessing ages, so she could've been a couple of years on either side of ten.

I would've crossed the street to talk to Burl, but after

telling my version of what I knew and saw more times than I would've liked to, I wasn't ready to repeat it. Instead, I stayed on the same side of the street as the haunted house and walked four blocks to my cottage.

I was tired when I got home and plopped down in bed hoping sleep would follow quickly. It didn't. Every time I started to drift off, visions of Chucky, Blackbeard, a mummy, a couple of ghosts popped in my head. I could handle those images. My confidence evaporated when I kept seeing the body from the pantry.

Chapter Four

Morning came earlier than usual after a restless night of mummies, Chucky, pirates, ghosts, and yes, a real dead body. Knowing the state of my kitchen pantry, going next door to Bert's Market for breakfast seemed like my best, possibly only, option to stop my stomach from an all-out revolt.

Bert's was usually quiet this time of day, so I hadn't expected to see anyone I knew; all the better after the event-filled evening and restless night. Of course, what we plan is seldom what we get.

I was halfway down the aisle when from across the room I heard the familiar voice of Burl Costello say, "Good morning, Brother Chris, how's this fine morning treating you?"

"Morning Preacher, wasn't expecting to see you this morning."

"I was going to give you a call. I saw you last night leaving the haunted house and wanted to touch base."

"I thought I saw you, but it was dark, so I wasn't sure."

He nodded. "I'm not one to stick my nose in something

that doesn't concern me but in a way this does. Being a shepherd, I need to keep my flock safe."

I smiled. "Preacher, I'm sure nothing is going to come out of the haunted house and steal the souls of the good people of Folly."

"Brother Chris, perhaps we should speak about it," he said as his eyes darted around the room.

Something was on his mind; something best not discussed in public.

"Want to go over to the house for coffee and donuts?"

Burl smiled. "A splendid idea. My favorites: donuts and good conversation."

"I'll get the donuts and try to come up with some good conversation."

I grabbed a box of prepackaged powdered sugar-covered donuts. We each drew a cup of complimentary coffee from the large urn, then headed to the counter. As I paid, I glanced at Burl, wondering why he was interested in last night's event and who the young girl was with him.

The short walk to the house was quiet with Burl matching me step for step but not saying anything. Strange, since he's usually talkative. I ushered him into the seldom-used kitchen where he attacked the box of donuts like he hadn't eaten in days. I ate two donuts to keep up with my guest. After all, I didn't want to be rude, or so I rationalized.

After he wiped flecks of powdered sugar out of his mustache, I said, "Preacher, what's on your mind?"

The question hung in the air as much as the smell of our coffee.

Burl reached for a third donut, then pulled his hand back. "Brother Chris, what do you know about the deceased individual? Know his identity?"

I leaned forward. "Charles and I stumbled into the situation. We were walking through the house and were startled like everyone else when we heard a scream that was more than someone frightened by a fake ghoul. There was a bunch of shouting and on the floor a body." I paused and waited for Burl to say something. He didn't, so I continued, "That's the end of the story. As far as I know, I'd never seen him and wish I hadn't last night." I again paused, but Burl remained silent. "Preacher, what's your interest? Do you know something about the death?"

Burl stirred his coffee as he looked at the donuts. He took a deep breath, then said, "It's about the young lady I was standing with when I spotted you. Do you know her?"

"Don't think so. I couldn't see her face that well, my eyes aren't as young as they used to be. Besides, at my age, I don't know many young people."

Burl chuckled, then said, "Brother Chris, I can appreciate that, the age part."

"Does she have something to do with what happened in the haunted house?"

He smiled, took a bite of donut, then said, "No, she was simply curious about what happened. Her name is Roisin. She moved to Folly from Minnesota with her family in May. We've become close in the last couple of months." He hesitated, then said, "She has a different way of looking at the world and is wise beyond her eleven years."

Not knowing what to say, but wanting to encourage him to talk, I said, "Does she and her family attend First Light?"

"No, I met her when she literally ran into me one afternoon in front of the Post Office. She was picking up her family's mail and flipping through a magazine when we collided." Burl chuckled. "Remember almost word-for-word what she said. 'So deeply sorry, sir. Didn't see you standing there. Please forgive my lack of observation.' She was more adult than many adults I know."

"It sounds like it."

"We stood there and spent nearly an hour talking about everything." Burl hesitated and laughed.

"What's so funny?"

"After she told me she was from Minnesota, she asked if I knew Minnesota has three times more white tail deer than college students. Of course, I didn't. I started to ask if she was related to Charles, the trivia collector."

"She sounds interesting."

"Quite. I met her mother, Shannon, the same day. I walked Roisin home to let her parents know where she'd been for so long."

"Oh," I said, not knowing what else to say.

"Brother Chris, the family follows a different spiritual path." He slowly took a sip of coffee, then added, "They're practicing Wiccans."

Visions of witches flying around the house on brooms or a witch with a group of flying monkeys flashed through my mind.

As if Burl could read my thoughts, he laughed. "It's not what you think. Wiccans are not the bad guys so many have made them out to be. While it's not Christian, it's a peaceful, nature-based religion."

"I'm not that familiar with the religion, Preacher."

"Not many are. Perhaps I could introduce you to Roisin and her family. Shannon owns Red Raven Herbs and Readings, a small business she runs out of their home. The dad's a lawyer."

"I'd like that."

A loud knock on the back door nearly brought me out of my chair.

Before I got to the door, Charles opened it, stuck his head in, and said, "Chris, have any suspects in our case?" He hesitated, looked at Burl, then as if nothing were unusual about me sitting in the kitchen sharing donuts with the preacher, said, "Hi Preacher. Didn't know anyone else was here."

Charles walked in the ever-shrinking kitchen, sat next to Burl, and looked at me for an answer.

"Charles, we don't have a case. We're aged citizens where one convinced the other to go to a haunted house and things that have nothing to do with us happened. End of story."

Charles said, "Ronald Reagan said, 'Facts are stubborn things.'"

"Gentlemen," Burl said, "I'll leave you to your discussion."

Charles said, "Preacher, you don't have to go."

"Brother Charles, if I don't prepare my sermon, I'll have an entire flock trying to stick me in the coffin that I hear is in the haunted house." He stood and looked toward the door. "I'm already a day behind."

I took his hint, thanked him for joining me for *breakfast*, and escorted him to the front door.

Leave it to Charles, aka the fount of presidential quotes, to be up bright and early itching to get started on an investigation, a preacher telling me there are witches among us, and here I am trying to peacefully have a donut and coffee after little sleep.

There's seldom a dull moment on Folly.

Chapter Five

After Burl left, Charles looked at the few remaining donuts, then to the empty counter near the sink, and said, "Man cannot live on donuts alone."

"Did a President say that?" I thought I knew the answer, but knowing Charles's penchant for quoting United States Presidents, I wouldn't put money on it.

"Probably, but I don't know who. You avoiding my question?"

"Which question?"

"You have any suspects?"

I was afraid that was the one. I started to respond when he held his hand in my face. "Hold that thought. Let's take a walk."

My back ached from tossing and turning all night, so it may have been one of Charles's better ideas. It was in the low sixties so I grabbed a light jacket and followed him out the back door, then toward Center Street, aptly named since it was the figurative center of the six-mile-long, half-mile-wide barrier island, and the center of commerce housing most of the island's restaurants and shops.

We reached Center Street when Charles said, "Well, suspects?"

"Charles, first, whatever happened is a matter for the police, not us. Second, even if there was the slightest chance it did involve us, how would I know anything about suspects? You were with me the entire time I was there. We left as soon as Detective Adair and Chief LaMond dismissed us."

We turned right on Center Street. Charles said, "Know where we're going?"

"The Dog."

"Wow, you're on your way to being nearly as good a detective as me. How'd you know?"

That was a much easier question than identifying suspects. "You said man, meaning you, couldn't live on donuts alone, so I figured you were hungry. The Dog is your favorite restaurant."

The Lost Dog Cafe, known by most residents and many vacationers as the Dog, was not only Charles's favorite restaurant, but mine as well. I'd eaten countless more meals there than in my cottage. The food was excellent, the atmosphere refreshing, and more importantly, they always had food, something that couldn't be said for my kitchen.

"Not bad. Now, how about suspects?"

"Charles, I said—"

"I know, I know, you don't have any. Wanted to give you a chance before I told you who I'm suspecting."

I'd have to wait until we were seated. We were escorted to a table in the center of the restaurant. It was often packed with people waiting for a table this time of day, but late October wasn't its busy season.

Amber, a server who'd been at the Dog since I moved to Folly, greeted us with a smile, a mug of coffee, and a question about what we wanted to order.

Charles returned her smile. "Dear, sweet Miss Amber, why don't you guess?"

"French toast for Chris, Loyal Companion for you."

No, Amber wasn't psychic. Those were the items we ordered roughly ninety-five percent of the time we were there for breakfast.

Charles smiled and said, "Excellent guess, Miss Amber."

Another no, neither of them consulted me on my menu choice. Sadly, I admit, they were right.

Amber left to put in our order and Charles returned to the topic I wanted to avoid.

"Chris, you know John or Bri Rice?"

"No. Who're they?"

"The J and the B of J&B Renovations. Husband and wife team."

"Okay, so what's J&B Renovations?"

"Mr. Unobservant, didn't you see the J&B job sign leaning against the haunted house?"

"Umm, no. Should I have?"

"Of course. It was there plain as day, right by the hose rack on the side of the house, turned so the words faced the house. How could you miss it?"

Could be because it was against the side of the house with the words facing the house so I couldn't read it. It would've been futile to say that, so I said, "Do you know them?"

"Nope."

"How do you know about them? I'm guessing since their sign was at the house, they had something to do with the renovations."

"You're catching on."

Before I asked what I was catching on, Amber returned with our meals and a question.

"Did you hear they found a body in the haunted house last night? A real body."

Charles looked at his plate, then at the server. "Miss Amber, glad you asked. Not only did we hear about it, we were there when it was discovered."

She shook her head. "Why doesn't that surprise me? What were you two geezers doing in the haunted house?"

"I was showing Chris what everyone's been talking about this Halloween season. Thought he needed to see what scares youngsters like you and me."

Amber had recently turned fifty, so I wouldn't put her in the youngster category, although she wouldn't hear that from me. Charles was nearly my age, so no comment was needed.

"Charles," Amber said, "since the customer is always right, I won't tell you what I think of your comment about us being youngsters. Sounds like you two stumbled into a horrible situation—again."

Charles said, "Amber, hear who the body belonged to?"

"Not yet. Nobody I've heard from has even said for certain what caused his death."

Charles said, "Any theories going around?"

She chuckled. "Old Mr. Musgrave said he must've been scared to death by a ghost in the house. Sally Denton figured it was a heart attack. If you ask me, they were guessing. None of our regular cop customers have been in, so I don't have an official version. You mean you don't know?"

"Not yet."

Two men at a table across the room waved in Amber's direction, so she headed their way.

"J&B Renovations," Charles said, answering the question I asked before Amber brought our food, "is in Mt. Pleasant. They do big and small jobs in the Charleston area. Hired by Dr. Robinson, the new owner of the house. It didn't look too bad on the outside, but from what I've heard needed a lot of work inside. Was taking longer than the owner thought it should, pissed him off royally. They're now supposed to be done November 1."

"Charles, if you didn't know the couple, how'd you learn about them? I doubt all that was on the side of the job sign facing the house."

"Last night after the senior citizen I was with went home to get his beauty sleep, I figured I couldn't learn anything about what happened holed up in my apartment, so I turned my trusty Schwinn around and peddled back to the haunted house. Stanley was getting ready to head home until I cornered him. A hundred clichés later, he told me everything I told you."

"Stanley didn't happen to know what happened to the guy did he?

"Nope."

"Did he know who he was?"

"Nope."

"Learn anything else from Stanley or anyone else there?"

"Nope. That's what our job is."

I thought, but didn't say, *nope.*

Chapter Six

Charles left the Dog to go to his apartment and get his bike so he could deliver a wetsuit for our friend Dude Sloan, owner of the surf shop. Charles's surf shop deliveries were limited to Folly and nearby areas since they were made on his bike. These deliveries along with helping a couple of restaurants clean during tourist season, and lending a hand to contractors who needed unskilled, seriously unskilled, help were ways Charles made enough money to live modestly.

Amber asked if I needed more coffee, but since I was about to float out the door, I declined. She also asked if I was okay after my trip to the haunted house. One of Amber's many attributes was her deep concern for people she'd friended over the years. After assuring her I was, I knew she wasn't convinced, but she was perceptive enough not to push.

She looked around to see if she was needed elsewhere in the restaurant, sat in the chair Charles had vacated, then said, "Jason and his girlfriend of the week went through the haunted house the night before you-know-what was found. What if he'd been the one to stumble on the body?"

Jason was Amber's twenty-one-year-old son who I'd first met when he was about the same age as Burl's friend Roisin. Amber and I'd dated a couple of years and she'd broken it off when Jason happened to walk in an apartment the same time I'd discovered a murdered woman. She was afraid I'd expose him to other dangerous situations. I'd thought that unlikely but understood her concern; a concern she was expressing now.

I explained how the body was in a room that wasn't part of the haunted house experience and reminded her Jason most likely wouldn't have seen the body even if he'd toured the house the night I was there. The look she gave me indicated she wasn't swayed by my explanation. A customer at the table behind us waved for the check, so Amber cut our conversation short to take care of the customer. I left money for my, and yes, Charles's breakfast on the table and told Amber I'd see her later.

Amber hadn't known the identity of the body, but if anyone did, it'd be Chief LaMond. So instead of heading home, I walked three blocks to the Folly Beach Department of Public Safety located in the salmon-colored City Hall. The Chief was sitting at her desk and partially hidden behind a stack of multi-colored folders. I stood in the doorway but was tempted not to disturb her since her expression reminded me of someone who'd watched their house get blown away in a hurricane.

The decision was made for me when Cindy looked up, saw me lurking, shook her head, then waved me in.

"Catch you at a bad time," I said, stating the obvious.

"Hell, Chris, why would you think that? All I'm doing is sitting here looking at photos of one of our cruisers. One that's two feet shorter than it was when Officer Dampier decided to chase a speeder out your road, then decided to swerve to avoid hitting a dog, then unintentionally, or so he said, decided to try to move a giant oak out of his way with the front of the car."

"Is Dampier okay?"

She tapped her finger on the photo. "He's much better than the tree and our newest patrol car. With that cheery image out of my head, what are you going to do to add more grief to my day?"

I smiled, hoping it'd be contagious, and said, "No grief, Chief. Thought I'd stop by to see how you were doing."

My smile wasn't contagious.

"Don't suppose you honestly think I believe that pile of crap?"

Instead of kicking me out, she motioned me to move two boxes off the chair in front of her desk, then to have a seat. I took it as a good sign.

"So, why'd you really come up here? Most sane citizens avoid this office."

"Curious what you've learned about the body in the haunted house."

"Anyone tell you what curiosity does to cats?"

"Sure, Chief. Glad I'm not a cat."

She stared at me. "Todd Lee."

"Todd Lee?"

"My first reaction to your curiosity comment was to tell you I didn't believe you, that you and probably Charles were nosing into something that's police business and none of yours. You would say of course you weren't nosing in, that you were there when the body was found, and simply curious. I'd tell you that was a crock. You'd give me that innocent smile you've perfected and wait for me to tell you what I knew."

"Chief, I'm—"

She leaned forward and waved her hand in my face. "I'm skipping all that. Todd Lee." She sat back in her chair and folded her arms across her chest.

It finally made sense. "Todd Lee was the victim."

"Wow, no wonder you claim to be a private detective."

"That's Charles, I'm merely a curious citizen."

"Right."

"So, who's Todd Lee?"

"Just told you. He's the body in the haunted house; the one that wasn't in a coffin."

Time to try another tact. "How'd you find out who he was?"

"Superior detective work."

"And?"

"Georgia driver's license in the wallet in his pocket."

"Excellent detective work."

"Smart ass."

"Yes ma'am. What else did you learn about Todd Lee?"

"Remind me why it's any of your business."

"Merely curious."

"I repeat, right."

I gave her one of my *innocent smiles* I wasn't aware I had and waited.

This time, she returned my smile. "Todd Lee turned forty-three nine days ago. Don't know how he celebrated his last birthday among the living."

"If his driver's license was from Georgia, what was he doing here?"

"Good question. In the condition he was in, he couldn't answer it, and no one else there knew him. So, no clue. The address on the license was in Savannah. Detective Adair is contacting police down there to see what they can find."

"Cause of death?"

"Hole in the heart, according to the coroner. Won't know for sure until the autopsy."

"Shot?"

"Nope."

"Knife?"

"Nope."

"Cupid's arrow?"

"Nope, wrong holiday."

I was out of options. "Then what?"

"No more guesses?"

"Nope."

She smiled. "I deserved that. You wouldn't guess it anyway. Ice pick."

"You're kidding."

She smiled again. "Nope."

"How long had he been dead?"

"Several hours before you showed up, so you're not a suspect, although if given time, I'd come up with something to charge you with."

Over the years, Cindy had threatened to have me arrested for everything from harassing a police chief, to being a pain in her rear. I ignored her comment.

"Was he killed in the house or put there after he was murdered?"

"Lividity would indicate that's where he took his last breath. If he was moved, it wasn't far, probably dragged."

"Did he have any connection to the haunted house?"

"No idea."

"Anything else?"

"Yeah, get out of here before I do something I could be arrested for."

I took the hint, thanked her, and left.

Chapter Seven

Charles was perched on his bicycle at the entry to the Folly Beach Department of Public Safety when I exited the building.

"What took you so long?" he said as he looked at his wrist, where, of course, no watch resided.

I ignored his comment. "What're you doing here?"

"Delivered a wetsuit to a man from France. He and his family are spending three months at Iguana House. Saw you heading in and figured you were interrogating the Chief about the dead guy. Found time in my busy schedule to wait for you."

The Iguana House is a rental property a block past the entrance to the Department of Public Safety. The house has an eclectic 1940s cottage look with a brightly colored exterior, not unlike many houses on the quirky island.

"Glad you could work it into your busy schedule," I said with a touch of sarcasm. "If you delivered a wetsuit, why is one in your basket?"

"Excellent question, resident of a land far from France. My new acquaintance looked at the wetsuit, held it up, and exclaimed something in his native tongue. I don't have to understand French to know he wasn't admiring my delivery."

"So why is it in your basket?"

"Apparently, it's the wrong size and for some reason beyond my understanding, he said I should have known that. I have the privilege of exchanging it for a larger size, a much larger size."

"Sorry. That where you're headed?"

"Nope. His condescending attitude didn't quite inspire a quick return with a suit that'd fit his ample belly. Know where I was headed next?"

I didn't ask how he thought I'd know. "Where?"

"Haunted house. Want a ride?"

I was much larger and heavier than any package he'd delivered for the surf shop, so I declined and said I'd meet him there.

I took the beach access path to West Ashley Avenue then the short walk to the haunted house. Charles had already parked and was talking to a man who appeared to be in his late forties, tall, maybe six-foot-six or taller, muscular, with dark brown hair. The image of Paul Bunyan came to mind.

"Chris, you know John Rice?"

"Don't believe so," I said, and extended my hand. "John, I'm Chris Landrum."

We shook hands and he said, "Pleased to meet you."

Charles said, "John owns J&B Renovations. They're doing the work on the house. I was telling him how we were here when the body was found."

John said, "Rough."

"Did you know the dead guy?" Charles said.

He was beginning his fishing trip.

Don't know," John said. "Who was it?"

I said, "Todd Lee."

Charles glared at me, no doubt because I hadn't told him what Cindy had shared.

"You're kidding," John said. "You sure?"

"I heard it from the Chief," I said, and added for Charles's benefit, "a few minutes ago. You know him?"

John waved at one of his workers entering a door to the lower level of the house. "Reggie, go ahead and fix the door. I'll be there in a few." He turned to Charles and me. "Sorry. What were you saying?"

"Did you know the dead guy?" Charles asked before I repeated the question.

"Umm, yeah. He came around looking for a job. I met him near where we're standing now. I needed help so I hired him. He worked about a week." He shook his head. "Not a good fit."

Charles said, "Why?"

"Don't get me wrong. He was a good worker but didn't take kindly to being told what to do or how to do anything. I couldn't have that, you understand. Told him I didn't need him any longer. Gave him an extra week's pay. I could tell he was borderline homeless. Felt sorry for the guy, but again, couldn't have his attitude on the jobsite, you understand."

Charles said, "When was the last time you saw him?"

John rubbed his chin. "Let's see. Must've been five, six days ago. Came to pick up his check. You sure it was him?"

"Afraid so," I said. "Is the haunted house interfering with your work here?" I asked to move the topic off the dead man.

"You know Fred Robinson, the owner?"

I shook my head and Charles said no.

"You're lucky. He hired my company to do an almost total renovation of the house. He said the house was perfect for him and his wife but needed work. Boy, did it ever. To be honest, it needed more than Robinson and I thought. We started and according to Robinson, we were so slow he took his wife on a European vacation just so he didn't have to fume about how slow we were progressing. Guy's a dentist and like most docs thinks he knows everything. We got in an argument or two early on." He smiled. "I told him he may know how long it takes to pull teeth and put on a crown but nothing about how long it took to renovate a house."

I said, "How'd he take that?"

"He bitched and moaned but took the hint. We came to an awkward agreement. I wouldn't pull teeth and he'd stay out of my way so I could get the job done. That and the haunted house."

Charles said, "What's that mean?"

Someone yelled for John from the door his worker entered earlier.

"Hang on, I'll be back."

He didn't know it would've taken a herd of elephants to pull Charles out of the yard when John had more to share.

Charles watched the contractor enter the house, then turned to me. "I think he killed the guy."

"Why?"

"Someone did. He's the first person we've talked to who knew the dead guy."

"Wow! What more proof do we need?"

"Smart ass."

"Too late," I said. "Cindy already called me that."

"Well, then—"

"Sorry guys," John said as he returned. "Where was I?"

Charles was quick with, "Telling us about the haunted house."

"When I was a little whippersnapper growing up in Charleston, I loved visiting Halloween haunted houses. Were some good ones, especially knowing the history of hauntings in Charleston. Led to other interests." He pointed to the house. "Anyway, first time I saw this house, I knew it'd make a perfect haunted house."

Charles said, "The dentist let you turn his future home into a haunted house?"

John chuckled. "Yes, course it helped that I promised a completion date the first week in November and reduced the price."

"Money talks," Charles said.

"It also gave me a chance to give back to the community and told him I'd do it in Dr. Fred Robinson's name. All the proceeds go to local charities. Think the good doctor saw dollar signs for his dental practice in the good publicity the house would get him."

Charles said, "Win, win."

John looked back at the house. "Don't know about the doctor winning considering there was a dead body found in there."

True, I thought.

"I'd better get back to work before I have a rebellion on my hands. Nice talking to you. If you need any renovation done at your places, give me a call." He handed each of us his business card then left us standing in the yard.

Charles held his hand in front of John. "Let me ask one more question."

"Sure, what?"

"The body was in the pantry."

"That's what I heard," interrupted John.

"We were told the pantry was locked and off limits to folks touring the haunted house. Any idea how it got there?"

John glared at Charles. "You accusing me of putting it there?"

"No, sorry, that's not what I meant. Wondering how the killer got in. Also, when we were going through the house, the kids in front of us were in the pantry. They found the body."

John slowly nodded. "The door had an old lock on it. Could've easily been opened with a credit card or a good shove. It's on the list of things we're upgrading."

"Oh," Charles said. "Makes sense. One more thing, did you provide all the scary stuff in the house like the fog machine, sound system for the spooky noises, other things?"

"Collected it over the years. Everything was mine except the coffin. Didn't have one of them laying around the house. Borrowed it from a funeral home in Mt. Pleasant." He looked at his watch. "Guys, I really have to run."

Chapter Eight

I walked beside Charles as he pushed his bike to the sidewalk across the street before turning toward Center Street. Once the haunted house was no longer in sight, he pulled off the sidewalk, glanced back in the direction of the worksite, and said, "Need any renovations done at your house? I know where you can get a good haunted house creating contractor."

His question didn't deserve an answer, so I said, "What'd you think of John?"

Charles glanced back toward the house again before saying, "Seemed okay. Thought it was a great idea doing the haunted house. It gave kids something to look forward to." He shrugged. "Who could find anything bad about giving the money raised to charity, especially the local charities. Admirable." He again glanced back.

"But?"

"But what?"

"You have that look on your face. Something's bothering

you about John other than fifteen minutes ago you thought he was the killer?"

"Can't put my finger on it. If I heard for the first time that a man who'd worked for me a few weeks earlier just so happened to turn up dead in my project, I wouldn't react calmly saying, 'Umm, yeah,' when asked if I knew him. He didn't act more shocked or traumatized than he would've if he learned someone stepped on a dandelion in his yard. Don't you think that was a serious underreaction?"

"Like he already knew the identity?"

"Yes, or was the guy who turned Todd dead. Seemed strange to me, that's all."

"Charles, we all react differently to bad situations. We don't know the man well enough to gauge his reaction."

"Why do you think I said I couldn't put my finger on it?"

"Anything else about him bother you?"

"Not really." Charles said. "What do you think he meant when he was talking about growing up visiting haunted houses and said something about how it led to other interests?"

"Don't know. Why didn't you ask him?"

"Was too surprised the dentist let John turn his new place into a haunted house."

"Sounds like the discount was too good to turn down."

"Whatever. Anyway, I still think there's something odd about John. Don't know if it's enough for him to kill Todd. Not ruling him out. Suppose I'd better get this itsy bitsy wetsuit back to Dude. Don't want to cause an international incident by not getting the Frenchie a chubby-sized one."

Charles was overestimating his influence in starting an

international incident, but I didn't want to keep him from his "job."

He peddled off after saying he'd talk to me later.

Later came quicker than I would've guessed. Charles called as I was taking the first bite of my "home-cooked" meal of a bologna sandwich, two slices of apple, and the plate colorfully adorned with a stack of Cheetos.

Instead of something normal people might say like, "Hey Chris," the first words out of his mouth were, "Bet you can't guess what Dude told me."

He was right, although, I'd wager Dude wouldn't have used a complete sentence telling him.

"He didn't have a wetsuit large enough for your French friend."

"No, I mean yes. He didn't have one large enough. He's going to call the guy, so I won't have to get yelled at in French. That's not what I'm talking about."

"Don't have to guess again, do I?"

"You're no fun."

"I agree, so what'd Dude tell you?"

"He asked if I knew who the dead guy was."

"Let me see if I have this right. You returned the wetsuit saying it wasn't large enough for your new friend, and Dude said, "Know who the dead guy was?"

"Not exactly. I told him about the wetsuit, and he said it took me a long time to get back. I told him about us visiting the haunted house, then talking with John. That's when Dude said, 'Who be dead bod?'"

"And you told him it was Todd Lee?"

"Duh, of course. Guess what he said."

I guessed, "Who be Lee?"

"Nope."

"Then what?"

He let out an audible sigh. "Have I told you lately you're no fun?"

Finally, a question I could answer.

"Yes, so what did Dude say?"

"Said, 'Be kidding. Me know Todd L.' He said it like he was shocked because it was someone he knew, unlike John's bland reaction."

"How'd Dude know him?"

"Said he came in the store asking if they were hiring. Of course, Dude didn't use all those words, but that's what he was trying to say."

"Don't suppose Dude hired him."

"You suppose right. Dude said Todd seemed nice, not pushy, not knowing everything like John said."

"People act different when they're trying to get a job. It doesn't mean Todd wasn't like John said he was once on the job."

"True."

"What else did Dude know about him?"

"Said he was sorry Todd be dead bod."

I didn't recall John saying that.

Chapter Nine

After a sleepless night followed by a day of running around, my body decided a visit to bed would be the best bet to avoid the haunting characters that'd visited me in my sleep the night before. Tonight, sleep came quickly and uninterrupted.

The phone was my alarm clock and I wasn't pleased.

"Brother Chris, how's this lovely morning treating you?"

"Fine I think, Preacher. What's up?"

"I was curious if you'd like to go with me this afternoon to visit Red Raven Herbs?"

"Who, where, when, what?" Jarred awake brain fog must've sent my vocabulary back to grade school.

He chuckled. "Guess I was vague. Red Raven Herbs is Shannon Stone's store. Remember, she's young Roisin's mom? You mentioned you'd like to meet the young lady and her family."

"Sounds good. Should I meet you there?"

"Unnecessary, Brother Chris. I'll swing by and pick you up around one."

With most of my friends I was the designated driver. It was pleasant having someone else offer to drive. I thanked Burl and said I'd see him then.

Walking next door to Burt's to get my morning coffee and unhealthy breakfast woke me enough to get my mind focused on meeting the Stone family. To my knowledge, I'd never known a Wiccan. I suspected what I'd seen on TV weren't the most accurate portrayals of the religion.

"That all you need?" asked Roger, one of Bert's personable clerks, as I took my cinnamon Danish to the register.

"Enough for now. I'll be back if I decide to fix supper."

"No reason to be rash on the supper fixin'. Enjoy a meal out; no cooking, no paper plate to throw away."

"Excellent suggestion," I said, as if there was a chance I'd cook a meal at home.

A weekly, okay, monthly cleaning while waiting on Burl kept most of my thoughts occupied. I didn't like going into a new situation with preconceived ideas, but I suppose it's human nature no amount of cleaning was going to sweep away. Burl wasn't a proponent of always early Charles's time schedule, so I was sitting on the porch a couple of minutes before one, when the preacher's Dodge Grand Caravan pulled in the drive.

"Are they expecting both of us?" I asked as I slipped in the van.

As Burl backed out of the drive, he said, "Yes, I talked to Shannon and Roisin this morning. Roisin is excited to meet you; suppose I've talked you up enough to impress a preteen."

"Thanks, I think."

"Shannon told me she and the kids will be happy to talk with us. Her husband is in Charleston and won't be back in time." He hesitated before saying, "These are good people, Chris. I know you'll go in with an open mind."

"I will, but what I don't understand is where you stand. Aren't their beliefs against God's teaching?"

"Brother Chris, meet them and after that if you still have questions, we can discuss it."

"Fair enough."

The remainder of the short ride was quiet except the music from a gospel CD with Burl humming along to "Amazing Grace." The house on East Huron Avenue was bordered on each side by large oaks and several shrubs isolating its residents from the neighbors. The small, concrete block, pre-Hugo single story cottage was painted an eye catching bright blue. The yard was impressive with flowers and plants everywhere. Even this late in the year it reminded me of a Monet painting.

We pulled in the drive when Burl said, "Brother Chris, not everyone treats others fairly. People can be quite cruel and ignorant. The Stones have had some issues—"

A raucous bark coming from a horse sized dog looking straight into my eyes through the passenger window interrupted Burl. I like dogs but I'd never seen one this large with so many big teeth—big teeth inches from my face.

Burl said, "That's Lugh."

"What's a Lugh and is it going to eat us?" I began to wish we'd brought Charles since there's never been a dog he didn't fawn over. At the least he would make a nice snack while Burl and I escaped.

A woman appeared on the front porch and yelled, "*Eist liom*!"

The massive canine loped to her and sat beside the attractive red headed woman. She smiled toward the van as the dog stared at her.

"It is safe," she said. "He will not harm you. He wanted to greet you his special way."

I said, "You sure?"

"Of course, if he wanted to harm you, he'd sneak up on you quieter than a speck of dust floating to the ground, then bare his teeth announcing displeasure. This is his cheery greeting. Shall we go have a pleasant conversation and a spot of tea?"

"Shannon, I'd like you to meet Brother Chris Landrum."

She gave a mini curtsy. "Good afternoon, Mr. Landrum. Welcome to my home. This big baby is Lugh. He's an Irish Wolfhound."

"Nice to meet you and Lugh. Please call me Chris."

"Come in out of this humidity. I'm still not used to this weather." She smiled. "Not sure I ever will be."

Stepping into the house was like walking through the door to a bygone era.

"Please have a seat in the parlor. I have a kettle on for tea."

"Roisin, our company is here," she said in the direction of what I assumed to be a bedroom.

Shannon left the *parlor* as if floating on air, Lugh followed her to the door then plopped down blocking the doorway.

Burl and I sat in what appeared to be antique wingback chairs. I said, "How often have you been here?"

"This is my third time at the house, it doesn't look like anything like you would think from the road."

I looked around and whispered to Burl, "Was thinking it doesn't look like anything from this century. The wallpaper is like something you'd see in England." I nodded toward the opposite wall. "That tapestry looks like it's over a hundred years old, same with the furnishings."

Burl glanced at the tapestry depicting a colorful garden scene. "Brother Chris, nature plays an important role in their lives, especially Roisin."

"You talking about me?"

I hadn't seen or heard our youngest hostess enter the room like magic as she appeared next to me.

In a quiet voice, she said, "Hello, I am Roisin. It's okay to stare, I know I'm a mini version of Mom."

"Nice to meet you, Roisin. I'm Chris," I said, hopefully covering being startled by her arrival.

Burl said, "Little Sister, how have you been? Where's that brother of yours?"

"Desmond is out back. He'll be in shortly." She rolled her eyes. "He likes to make a grand entrance."

Shannon appeared in the doorway to the kitchen. "Roisin, please help serving. Chris, would you like a scone with your tea? I know Burl enjoys them."

"Yes, please."

Burl took a cup of tea off the silver platter and put a scone on a matching saucer, then said, "I brought Chris so he could meet your family and learn about your beliefs. He has an open mind; unlike some you've encountered."

Shannon set the platter on a table in the corner of the room, took a seat on an upholstered Victorian sofa, and said, "Burl, any friend of yours is welcome here. We have had a few issues but that's nothing new. Being Wiccan, we're occasionally viewed as evil people worshiping the devil or practicing the Dark Arts."

I said, "I admit, I know nothing of Wiccan beliefs."

Shannon took a sip of tea, glanced around the room, before saying, "If you look around you will see objects that may seem strange or out of place. These are a few of the implements used in our religion." She looked across the room. "On the table against the wall are candles, salt, incense, water, herbs, and crystals. It's the family altar."

Roisin said, "Mr. Chris, those things represent the four elements. Wicca is the love of life and nature. Everything in nature should be treated with the utmost respect." She smiled. "People see me walking around talking to animals and things in nature. They look at me like I'm crazy. Mom says they are out of touch with things our natural world can offer." Her smile turned to a frown. "They lack the respect that should be given. I have been taught everyone has the right to their ideas and beliefs."

Shannon said, "That's my eleven-year-old, going on thirty. She can get a bit overzealous when someone shows interest, but her words are true."

I smiled. "Shannon, Roisin, Preacher Burl tells me Red Raven Herbs is your online store. What do you sell?"

"Herbs, crystals, and bath salts online and by word of mouth over here." Her voice lowered. "While I know it's prohibited on Folly, I occasionally do card readings, by appointment, and only for people I know. Spells are also performed if requested."

"Spells, like curses?"

An uneasy giggle broke out from Shannon and her mini me daughter. I wasn't sure if it made me feel better or worse. Nothing witty came to mind to defuse what I might have started so I took a bite of scone and waited for what would come next, praying it wasn't a curse.

Shannon shook her head. "Curses, no that would be going against what we practice, harm none and the law of threefold. "The spells I was referring to would be for love, health, peace, and so on."

"I didn't mean to offend."

Shannon leaned forward and patted my arm. "No offense taken. This is how people learn about others, asking questions and being open to the answers. We were aware of the challenges that might arise when moving here from Minnesota leaving the community that was like family. That is life and life is everchanging."

I said, "I would never have guessed your accent was Minnesotan."

She surprised me with a full throated laugh. "Yes, by way of Kilkenny, Ireland. I moved to Minnesota in the late nineties. I met, fell in love with Mike, the rest is history."

I said, "Why Folly?"

"Mike received an excellent job offer from a law firm in Charleston that he'd heard about from a friend from law school. They needed a medical attorney. The company offered us access to a nice house in Charleston, but I couldn't see the family being at peace in the big city. Folly seemed so inviting and laid back. We could not resist. Found this house our first day on the island. The Goddess blessed us, and here we are."

Burl said, "Brother Chris, that sounds like how most of us got here. You, me, now the Stone family. Folly has benefited from our diverse presence."

"You are very kind, Burl," Shannon said.

"Kind, and a weaver of bologna. Folly is more eclectic than anything we can provide."

We shared our experiences discovering Folly and the weather in October, then I said, "Shannon, Roisin, thank you both for your hospitality. We won't take up more of your afternoon. The scones were great as well as the conversation."

Burl patted his stomach. "Good food and conversations are this preacher's vices. As usual, I've had a wonderful time. Sister Roisin, we still on for our walk to the marsh this week?"

"Of course, don't forget your notebook so I can teach you more fauna."

Lugh rose and walked over to the chairs before I was fully standing. For his size, I was amazed how quietly he moved. Burl petted the dog as I shook Shannon's hand and smiled at Roisin.

On the way to the door, a room to the left caught my eye. On a small round table in the middle of the room there was a lit candle and a variety of metal and wooden tools including an ice pick. I would've sworn the door to the room had been closed when we passed it upon arriving.

On the way to the van, Burl said, "Brother Chris, I believe that went well. Did you enjoy yourself?"

"Yes, but I thought Roisin's brother was going to come in."

"Desmond has a way about him."

Turning to walk to the passenger side of the car I nearly ran into a young Ozzy Osbourne look alike. He was dressed in black but wasn't giving off the good vibes of Johnny Cash.

The young man, roughly sixteen, I would guess, said,

"Sorry I'm late, had something that needed to be done. Did you find out everything you wanted to know about the freaky family living there? He pointed to the house, his house. "Sorry there were no coffins or dead goats. Guess it was boring."

"Desmond, this is Chris Landrum, a good friend of mine," Burl said, ignoring the young man's snarky comments. "We wanted to visit; missed you not being there. We have a few minutes if you'd like to talk."

"No. I'm sure you have all the answers to your questions, besides your friend looks a little pale."

We pulled out of the drive and Burl went back to humming gospel and my mind processed the afternoon's events. Shannon seemed pleasant and I saw why Burl adored Roisin, but I couldn't shake the feeling of dread when looking into Desmond's crooked smile. He looked out of place in the beautiful garden in front of the little blue cottage. He'd look more at home in a mausoleum or yes, a haunted house.

Chapter Ten

"Have I got a deal for you," Chief LaMond said to begin her early morning call.

"Morning, Cindy," I said in an attempt to add a glimmer of civility to the conversation. "And what might that be?"

"Head to the Dog and I'll let you buy me breakfast."

I smiled and said, "Wow! How lucky can a guy get?"

"Wise reaction. You on your way?"

I told her I'd be there in ten minutes, knowing Cindy had something to share or wouldn't have called.

It took me closer to fifteen minutes, but Cindy wasn't as anal about being prompt as Charles, so I didn't worry about being castigated for being late. The fog was so thick on the drive over, I could barely see fifty feet in front of me.

Cindy was at a table near the front of the restaurant tapping on her phone and sipping coffee. She saw me enter, placed the phone face down on the table, pointed her coffee mug at me, and said, "Get lost in the sea fog?"

Okay, she was slightly time sensitive, still far from Charles's level.

Amber was quick to the table with a mug of coffee. She chuckled. "Chief said to get you anything you want. Said you were buying her breakfast so to treat you nice."

"Thanks, Amber. Chief LaMond is sweet like that. Think I'll have French toast."

Cindy said, "Told you so, Amber."

"That's why you're Chief," Amber said and headed to put in my order.

Since Cindy extended the *generous* invitation, I took a sip of coffee and waited for the reason for the invite.

"So, aren't you going to ask what I've learned about the murder?"

"Figured you'd tell me when you're ready."

"Okay, here goes. This is everything I know about the murder." She held up her right hand and touched her forefinger to her thumb forming a circle, or more accurately, a zero.

"Nothing?"

"Correct, Mr. Senior Citizen. I know nothing more than I did the last time we talked. I had a worthless call this morning from Detective Adair. He'd contacted police in Savannah in an attempt, feeble attempt, to find out where the late Todd Lee lived. They found no record of anyone by that name ever living in their historic city: no speeding tickets, no parking tickets, not even cited for jaywalking. Add to that, none of my officers recall having contact with Mr. Lee." She shook her head. "Chris, I'm beginning to believe Todd Lee was another one of the ghosts in the haunted house."

"Didn't his drivers' license list an address?"

"Excellent point. Yes, it did."

"So why couldn't the police have learned he lived there?"

"Another excellent point. They probably could have if it weren't for the fact the address on his license belonged to an empty lot. Empty now, apparently there was a small building there at one time, a building demolished in the 1940s, long before Todd Lee was born. See what I mean about him being a ghost?"

"Yes. Sorry, Cindy. Anything else about Lee?"

Amber arrived with my breakfast before Cindy responded. I slathered syrup on the French toast and waited for the Chief to enlighten me as to why I was there.

"Chris, I'm from the mountains of East Tennessee; didn't pay much attention in school. I'm not big on history and all that old stuff, but I seem to recall some famous guy saying something about folks who fail to learn from the past are condemned to repeat it, or something like that."

"Chief, I'm impressed. Think it was George Santayana."

"Thought that was a rock band."

"That's Carlos Santana."

"Damn, Chris, you're getting worse than Charles."

"That's a low blow. Remind me again of your point."

"Haven't told you the first time. My point is history tells me you, Charles, and possibly a few other misfits you hang with, have a way of nosing into things that aren't your business. So, I'm learning from the past that you're going to do the same thing when it comes to the untimely death of Todd Lee. How am I doing?"

I smiled. "Chief, I wouldn't call it nosing into his death, but there are a couple of things we've learned that you and

Detective Adair might not be aware of. A couple of days ago—"

She interrupted, "I love being right."

I took a sip and waited for her to finish gloating so I could continue.

"Okay, I feel better. What did you learn?"

I told her about meeting John Rice and what he'd said about Todd Lee working for him a week, why he'd been fired, and how Todd had returned to get his paycheck. Cindy started to give me grief about visiting the haunted house and, in her words, interrogating John Rice. She stopped mid sentence saying it wasn't worth her breath telling me I shouldn't have done it.

She jotted a couple of things in her notebook before asking if I thought Rice could've had something to do with the death.

"Nothing that was apparent. He didn't appear upset Lee was dead or that the body was found in the house he was renovating, but we each react differently to things, so it could mean nothing."

"I'll share that with Adair. He'll probably want to talk to Rice again. Anything else?"

"Not about the murder, but do you know the Stone family?"

"Blue house, East Huron?"

I nodded.

"What about them?"

"Preacher Burl took me to meet them yesterday."

Cindy took a sip of coffee, looked at the front of her phone, and said, "So?"

"Late for something?" I asked, noticing it was the second time she'd glanced at her phone.

"Yeah, but don't change the subject. Why ask if I knew the Stones?"

"Thought they were interesting."

"Because they're witches?"

I sighed. "Wiccans."

"Witches, Wiccans, whatever."

"What else do you know about them?"

"Mom runs an Internet herbs company out of the house. Dad's an attorney."

"Anything else?"

"About three months ago, the dad, think his name's Mike, called to file a report. Seems some jackass left a broom leaning against their front door with a note saying something like, 'Hop on this and fly out of town. Your kind ain't wanted here.'"

"What'd you do?"

"Officer Bishop caught the call, took the note as evidence, apologized to the head witch, excuse me, Wiccan, and said we'd keep a closer eye on the house."

"How'd he react?"

"He's an attorney. Told Bishop he knew there was nothing more she could do and thanked her for coming. He was a hell of a lot nicer than I would've been. Bishop said she apologized again for them having to put up with some narrowminded jackass. Don't think she put it exactly like that but should've." Cindy took another sip, stared at me, before saying, "See if I have this right. You asked if I knew them because they were interesting?"

"Yes. I thought of them because Preacher Burl was outside the haunted house the night the body was found. He was with the Stones' young daughter Roisin. That's all."

"Interesting. Hmm, if you say so. Regardless, I'm late for a fun filled meeting with his honor the Mayor."

I wished her luck with the meeting; she said she'd need it.

After she left, I wondered if I should've mentioned the ice pick at the Stones' cottage.

Chapter Eleven

I was finishing my coffee while wondering why I didn't have something better to think about than a murder, when a shadow fell across the table. Looking up from my mug, I was greeted by the smiling face of John Rice.

"Chris, right?"

"Correct, Mr. Rice."

"Call me John. Mind if I join you if you're not too busy?"

I smiled. "Too busy, no. I'm retired so I've no place to rush off to."

Amber noticed the addition to the table and returned to clear the plates and ask John if he needed a menu.

"No menu," he said with a smile. "I'd like a bagel with cream cheese, bacon, and iced tea, if that wouldn't be too much of a burden on such a pretty lady."

Amber rewarded him with the kind of smile people use when faced with a nice yet back handed comment. She picked up my plate and pointed to my mug. I nodded before she headed to the kitchen.

John said, "Other than my crew, I don't know many folks on the island. Some days eating alone isn't much fun."

"If you'd arrived a couple of minutes earlier, you could've met another Folly resident, Chief Cindy LaMond, our number one crime fighter."

"I saw her leave."

His tone was more like he was waiting for her to leave before he came in, or I could be looking for ulterior motives where none exist—in other words, becoming Charles. Laughing to myself, I thought about the belief that couples start to look and act alike after being together for a long period. My internal monologue must've lasted too long when I realized the room was eerily quiet.

I said, "Maybe you can meet her next time. How's the renovation coming?"

"Little behind schedule,but that's expected since there was so much rot and damage we couldn't see when estimating a completion date. Still think we'll make it on time." He looked toward the door before turning back to me. "If you don't mind, I'd rather not talk shop."

I nodded. "No shop talk it is."

Amber arrived with John's food, drink, and my refill. She smiled at me, then headed to another table without a word.

John took a bite, a sip of tea, then looked at me like it was my turn to speak.

I took the hint. "The other day when Charles asked why you promoted the house to the owner as becoming a haunted house you said something about liking them as a child."

He smiled. "Halloween was my favorite time of year. Went to a bunch of haunted houses, a haunted forest or two. Those were in my younger, much younger days."

"I think you said it led to other interests."

He looked at me like I'd asked a trick question, before saying, "Paranormal activity, my true passion besides my wife. Luckily, she's into it as much as I am."

Casper the ghost floated up in my mind, not the friendly one, but a headless version. Halloween was becoming my least favorite time of year.

"Paranormal, like ghost hunting?"

"You might say that. Growing up in Charleston with its prolific afterlife community either gets a youngster interested or repulses him." He chuckled. "I'm in that former group. Bri is from Savannah, another paranormal hotbed, so we immediately hit it off."

"Interesting," I said, although not very.

"We host ghost tours and paranormal activity research, founded Lowcountry Paranormal Investigations."

"Oh," I inarticulately said. "Sounds like a fascinating business."

"Yes, Charleston is filled with paranormal activity from the old slave market to many of the historic downtown buildings, not to mention nearby plantations."

"I'm not originally from here, so I wasn't reared knowing much about it."

"Ah, it's everywhere, my friend." He pointed his glass at me. "The dead don't hurt you. It's the living, although Bri and I've come across some instances where the dearly departed weren't so dear. Oh well, just curiosity on both parts, the living and the dead."

He smiled as he took a large bite. He looked at me like

he was trying to get my take on the strange direction our conversation had headed. I was never a believer in the supernatural or hauntings, so sitting across from someone who did and talked about it like others did about the weather seemed odd.

"Interesting," I repeated. "I guess you don't think a ghost killed Todd Lee?"

John laughed so loud customers at a table behind us looked our way to see what was so humorous.

He lowered his voice. "We've seen little evidence of ghosts in the Robinson house, so my guess would be it wasn't one of them that took his life. Was stabbed if the rumor going around's true."

"You'd said he was a pain to work with. Did he have conflicts with anyone on your crew or was he close with someone? I was wondering since he was back in the house after you'd let him go."

"Not sure if he got along with any of my guys. If I had to pick one who had the most beefs with him, it'd be Nathan Davis, one of my carpenters. He and Todd had a few heated words." He took another sip before continuing. "Todd tried to tell Nathan the best way to measure lumber, something stupid and none of his concern. Nathan has been a carpenter all his life and had worked for me for years."

"Nathan didn't like the newbie telling him how to do his job."

"Would you?"

"Did it ever get physical?"

"Pretty sure it would've if I hadn't stepped in. Funny though."

"Funny?"

"Nathan called him a world class pain in the ass. Todd

went off like he'd been slapped in the face. He was ready to stomp on Nathan."

"Was Todd just bullying someone smaller than he was?"

"Nope, Nathan is a big, burly guy. I was concerned about my new hire getting his clock cleaned. Can't have that on my jobsite."

"Fired him after that?"

"Next day. I wanted to give him a second chance, but he came in the next morning more pissed than the day before." John shook his head and stared at the table.

Could he be wishing he could've done more for the late Mr. Lee? I had a feeling our conversation was about to end, and I wasn't sure where I'd hoped our discussion had been headed in the first place. What I did have was the name of another person who knew the victim; not only knew but had run ins with him. The pool always seems to get deeper and deeper the harder you look. For good or bad, I had someone else Charles could claim was the killer.

My thoughts were interrupted when John said, "I've got to get back to work. Sorry to have invited myself to breakfast."

"No need to apologize."

As he left money on the table for his meal and headed to the door, I couldn't help thinking he seemed like a genuinely nice person. Unusual interests, but nice. He runs two businesses with his wife, donates to charities and is concerned about his employees, and even about a man who worked for him a week, one he didn't particularly like. So, why was I feeling he's holding something back?

Then what about Nathan Davis? Could he have something to do with Todd's demise? With so many questions bouncing around in my head, I should leave before someone else decides to join me.

The drive home cleared my head enough to realize I'd have to tell Charles what I'd learned. He'll belittle my interrogation skills, but that's okay, all in a day's work for one retired citizen who happens to have a friend named Charles Fowler.

Chapter Twelve

That evening, a three block walk to Cal's Country Bar and Burgers, commonly called Cal's, might get my mind off the haunted house and who might've killed Todd Lee. Besides, it'd been a few weeks since I visited the bar's owner. I'd known Cal since he settled on Folly nearly a decade ago after spending most of his seventy five years traveling the South singing his brand of country music at any venue that'd have him. I was honored to call him a friend. We'd gotten better acquainted earlier this year when he learned he'd fathered a child fifty plus years ago. To put it mildly, Cal was traumatized when the son he didn't know he had, moved to Folly to be closer to his dad. I'd become Cal's sounding board.

I entered the bar to the sound of Patsy Cline singing "I Fall to Pieces" from the classic Wurlitzer jukebox. The jukebox wasn't the only classic thing in the room. The tables, chairs, flooring, walls, and Cal would all fit that definition. Mid October wasn't peak season and only two of the dozen tables were occupied, plus two people seated at the bar along the right side of the room.

Cal was behind the bar setting a beer bottle in front of each of the nearby customers. He was wearing a Stetson that's been with him since Lyndon Johnson was President, a long sleeve sweatshirt with an image of Hank Williams Senior on the front, and a wide smile when he saw me at the entry.

He held up an empty wineglass, I nodded, he turned to grab a bottle of Cabernet off the backbar, filled the glass with a heavy pour, and pointed to a vacant table near the front of the room.

"See Charles on your way in?" Cal said as he folded his six-foot-three, slim body in the chair opposite me.

"No. Was he here?"

"Trying to find you. I wanted to remind him he had one of those modern day inventions called a cell phone that'd probably be easier finding you than traipsing all over town."

"Cal, you just learning you can't tell Charles anything?"

"You betcha."

Before Cal elaborated, my phone rang with Charles's name appearing on the screen. I pointed the phone at Cal so he could see who it was, then answered.

"You know you're not at home, Loggerhead's, Cal's, Rita's, or Planet Follywood?" Charles said instead of hello.

"Wrong."

"Wrong, what?"

"I'm at Cal's enjoying a glass of wine and talking to Cal."

"You weren't, oh, never mind. On my way."

The phone went dead.

"Cal, how about grabbing a Bud for Charles."

He tipped his Stetson and headed to the bar.

Roger Miller was singing "King of the Road" when Cal returned with Charles's beer.

"Hear you and Charles were playing like you were kids going through the haunted house when the stiff got himself discovered."

"Who said that?" I asked, although not surprised Cal would know.

"One of the kids named Charles. He also said the two of you were going to figure out who killed the guy."

I shook my head. "It's in the capable hands of the police."

Cal laughed then said, "Of course it is. Then I guess you wouldn't be interested in talking to the guy sitting at the end of the bar."

I glanced at the bar. The person Cal was referring to was in his mid forties, long black hair, burly, and appeared tall, although I couldn't tell for sure since he was seated.

"Who's he?"

"Name's Nathan Davis, works on the crew renovating the house that's temporarily haunted."

The name sounded familiar, but it took me a few seconds to remember he was the person John Rice said had conflicts with the murder victim.

"Why would I want to talk to him?"

"Charles said no one knew why the guy was killed in the house. Nathan, prefers Nate, is here most days after work. Nice fellow, doesn't get loud or obnoxious, pays his tab, doesn't pick fights, but is a world class bitcher."

"He say something about the body?"

Charles came in the door; Cal waved him over, then said, "I'll leave you two Hardy Boys to detectin'." Cal tipped his Stetson toward Charles then headed to the bar before answering my question about Nathan who prefers Nate.

Charles took a long drag on the beer, not asking if it was for him, set his Tilley on the corner of the table, and said, "So, where were you when I was in here a little while ago?"

"Hiding from you under the table."

His eyes narrowed. "You're kidding, right?"

"Yep. Was hiding behind the bar. Why were you looking for me?"

"Funny. Haven't heard from you in a couple days. Wanted to confab about our plan to catch a killer."

Before we could *confab*, there were a couple of things I had to share then brace for a ton of grief he'd give me for not telling him sooner. I took a deep breath, a sip of wine, then began sharing about my visit to the Stone family. As predicted, Charles stopped me with a hand in my face.

"Why wasn't I invited?"

I repeated what I'd already said about Burl inviting me since I'd expressed interest in meeting them the day after the haunted house fiasco. I didn't think I needed to point out the invitation was to me, not Charles and me.

He sighed before saying, "Go on. What else did I miss—miss because I wasn't invited?"

I got as far as mentioning Lugh before he interrupted with a barrage of questions about the dog's name, breed, and size. It took the rest of Charles's beer before I reached the end of the story.

"What'd the Stone family have to do with the murder?"

"Probably nothing, although it was an interesting coincidence that Todd Lee was killed with an ice pick and that there was one in their house."

"Like there is in most every house or garage on Folly."

"That's why I said it was interesting, not necessarily relevant."

He made a couple more *feeling sorry for himself for not being invited utterances* before calming. I knew it was temporary then began telling him about meeting with John Rice and what he said about being a paranormalist and how one of his employees, Nathan Davis, had conflicts with the dead guy.

Lightning might not strike twice in the same place, but volcanos can. So can Charles. I thought he was going to fly out of his chair, before pounding his beer bottle on the table, rolling his eyes, and nonverbally doing a volcano erupting imitation.

I sat back, listened to Johnny Horton singing "Sink the Bismarck" and waited for glimmers of sanity to reenter Charles's body. It was an uncomfortable but necessary wait.

Charles finally calmed, quicker than usual, a sign of maturity, or possibly lack of energy attributable to aging. Regardless of the reason, I was pleased.

He took another sip, then said, "Other than not thinking about your friend while galivanting all over town investigating the murder, anything else you haven't shared?"

"Only one more thing, see that guy sitting at the end of the bar?"

Charles pivoted toward the bar. "Yes."

"Know who he is?"

"No, who?"

"Nathan Davis."

The former volcanic eruption morphed into a laser guided missile. Charles was out of his chair and headed to the bar before I could ask what he was doing. He pulled the barstool closest to Davis and started talking to the unsuspecting interviewee. Two minutes later, Charles, along with his new friend were headed to my table.

"Chris, meet my new buddy Nate Davis. Would you believe Nate is working with J&B Renovations, that's the company fixing up the haunted house?"

I could believe it since it's what I told Charles five minutes earlier. I shook Nate's hand and Charles pointed for him to join us.

"Chris, I told Nate you were buying the drinks. That okay?"

"Sure," I said, as if I had a choice.

"Thanks," Nate said, "Charles told me you were in the haunted house when someone found Todd."

I nodded. "You know him?"

I could play Charles's game.

"I guess. He worked with us about a week before John, he's the company's owner, wised up and canned him."

Charles leaned closer to Nate. "How come?"

Nate began peeling the label off his beer bottle. "Because he's a first class asshole."

Charles said, "Sounds like you didn't get along."

Nate glared at Charles. "No, but I didn't kill him."

Charles smiled at Nate. "Of course not. Just wondering why you think he was an asshole."

"He was a know-it-all. Knew everything about construction. The rest of us were idiots, unable to operate a screwdriver, according to him."

"Sounds like a prince to work with," Charles said.

"You can say that again. Not only did he know everything, he kept telling me how he wouldn't need his crappy job much longer."

"What'd that mean?" Charles asked.

"Don't know; didn't like him enough to ask. He'd tap his head with a finger and say something about a secret he knew that was going to make him rich." He looked around the room then said, "Fellas, I may've killed him myself, if somebody didn't beat me to it."

Cal moved beside Charles. "Anything else for you guys?"

"Another beer for my friend here?" Charles said as he pointed at Nate.

"Anything else?"

"Not yet, Cal. Chris is picking up the tab."

Cal left to get Nate another drink and increase my indebtedness.

Charles turned his attention back to Nate. "Any idea who killed him?"

"No."

"Know why he was killed in the haunted house?"

"Nope. He had no business being there."

"How long have you worked for J&B?" I asked to move the discussion away from the murder.

"Going on five years. Good company to work for; pay's good. John's a little rough on his employees, but Bri's a doll, can swing a hammer with the best of us although you couldn't guess it seeing her blond ponytail sticking out behind her pink hardhat." He smiled.

"Sounds like a good job," I said, not knowing anything to add.

"Biggest problem is clients, always wanting the job done faster than possible, wanting us to slash costs."

Cal arrived with Nate's beer, and again asked if we needed anything. I said no; Charles shook his head. Cal left to see if the couple at a table by the small bandstand in front of the room needed anything.

"How's—umm, what's his name, Chris?"

"Dr. Robinson," I said, assuming he meant the haunted house's owner.

"Yeah, how's Dr. Robinson to work for?"

"I'd put him in the pain in the ass category, although I don't have to deal with him directly. John has that pleasure."

Charles said, "What's his problem?"

"Let's just say, I wouldn't want him working with a drill in my mouth. The boy's got a temper combined with a snooty attitude."

Charles said, "He know Todd Lee?"

"Lee was only there a week, thank goodness. Let's see. Don't know about the damned dentist knowing Lee, but think his wife, believe her name's Erika, may've been in the house once that week. Why?"

"Curious," Charles said.

Also known as nosing around, trying to catch a killer. Hopefully, Nate didn't know Charles well enough in the few minutes since they'd met, to figure that out.

Nate looked at his watch. "Wow, where does the time go? Fellas, I've got to be at work early in the morning. Umm, thanks for the beers, Chris."

He pushed his chair back, thanked me again, before heading to the door.

Charles watched him go, turned to me, and said, "See, Chris, that's why you need me with you when you're trying to catch a killer."

"What do you think about Nate?" I asked, ignoring his critique.

Charles took a sip, nodded, then said, "Think he's got a thing for a blond with the pink hardhat. Think he wasn't president of the Todd Lee fan club. Think he's not adding the Robinsons to his Christmas card list."

"Think he killed Todd Lee?"

"Hell if I know."

And that's why I need him with me when trying to catch a killer?

Johnny Cash's distinct voice filled the air with "Oh Lonesome Me."

Chapter Thirteen

It'd been several days since I'd seen Barbara Deanelli, the lady I'd been dating for a little over two years. She owned Barb's Books, a used bookstore on Center Street. After a lazy morning around the house, it was time to rectify that situation. The temperature was in the upper end range for late October and the store was two blocks from my cottage, so I couldn't come up with a good reason not to walk. The store was housed in a space I'd rented when I had a photo gallery, a lifetime dream that'd become a nightmare when I learned photos weren't as popular to the buying public as food, medicine, and lottery tickets.

Although used books were vastly more in demand than my photos, other than Barb, I was the only person in the attractively decorated store. Barb was my height at five-foot-ten, thin with short black hair. She greeted me with a smile, a kiss, and an invitation for a drink of my choice, if it was a soft drink, water, coffee, or wine. I followed her to the small backroom and said coffee sounded good. She grabbed a pod from a stainless steel rack and plopped it in the Keurig machine before getting a bottle of water for herself.

"What brings you out?" she asked, knowing it wasn't to buy a book.

"Hadn't seen you for a while so I thought I'd stop by and enjoy your company for a few minutes."

"That's sweet if I believed it."

"It's true."

"Okay," she said with a skeptical look. "Then have a seat and enjoy the coffee and my company."

She rolled her chair close to the door so she could see customers venturing in.

I took a sip and said, "Hear about the dead body found in the haunted house the other night?"

"Aren't there always dead bodies in haunted houses?"

I smiled. "This was a real one."

"I know," she said as she continued to look to the front of the store. "Was joking. I'd be a poor example of a Folly resident if I missed hearing something like that."

"Did you hear Charles and I were there when it was found?"

Her head jerked in my direction. "You've got me there. I hear when men get old, really old, they regress to their childhood. That what you and your buddy were doing?"

I didn't remind her she was a mere two years younger than I. "No. Charles wanted me to experience what kids enjoy nowadays."

"And it just so happened on the same night a body was visiting?"

"Afraid so."

"Why doesn't that surprise me?"

"Bad luck."

"Speaking of bad luck, know what happened, who he was, and who killed him?"

"Can answer two of the three. Name was Todd Lee, killed by an ice pick through the heart. Ever hear of that?"

She shook her head. "I've had the privilege, speaking sarcastically, of knowing a few murderers in my day, but never one using an ice pick. Who's Todd Lee?"

Barb had been a successful defense attorney in Pennsylvania before moving to Folly a little over two years ago after going through a divorce.

"Don't know much about him, nobody appears to. He worked for a week on the crew renovating the structure they're using for the haunted house. Don't know where he lived or why he was killed. Do you know John or Bri Rice?"

"Don't believe so. Who're they?"

I shared what little I knew about the contractors.

"Do they know anything about him other than he worked for them a short period of time?"

I shook my head and added, "Don't know Nate Davis, do you? He works on the J&B crew and had argued with the dead guy."

Her gaze narrowed. "You and Charles sticking your noses in police business again?"

"Not really."

"Not to parse words, but *not really* isn't the same as no."

"We have no reason to butt in."

"Again, not the same as no."

Time to change the subject.

"Do you know Mike or Shannon Stone?"

"Finally, a question I can answer. Don't know Mike but Shannon comes in occasionally; so does their son, believe his name's Desmond. Then there's little Roisin. She's something else. How do you know them?"

"Burl Costello took me to meet them the other day. Mike wasn't home, but I met the rest. They seem like a nice family."

She grinned. "Burl the minister took you to meet a Wiccan family?"

I laughed. "Seems Roisin friended Burl. What did you mean by she's something else?"

A customer came in before Barb responded. She went to see if she could help and I leaned back, enjoyed the coffee, and a piece of Halloween candy from a bag on the table. A few minutes later, Barb returned.

"Can you believe I didn't have a single book on the Samburu tribe in Northern Kenya?"

"I can't believe someone was looking for one."

"Well, she was; I didn't and lost another customer. Where were we?"

"Roisin Stone."

"That young lady is as sharp as some of the attorneys I worked with; more inquisitive, too. She comes with Shannon and regardless which section Shannon goes to, Roisin darts the other direction and starts pulling books, parks herself on the floor, and flips through them like she's reading whatever they're about. She came in once with her brother who's as different from her as a tree to a turnip. If I had a Goth section, that's where he'd hang out."

"I only talked to him for a minute but you're right. Burl said Mike was a medical lawyer. How's that different from what you practiced?"

"Attorneys can't specialize in specific areas while in school, but as you know, many find a niche in which to focus when making a living. The ones who gravitate toward medical law often represent plaintiffs who've been injured due to alleged malpractice or hospital errors. Of course, in the wonderful world of law where there are at least two sides to everything, they go against other medical attorneys defending the docs or the hospitals."

"Any attorney can claim to be a medical attorney?"

"Yes. That's why potential clients should check an attorney's track record before signing on as a client."

"Makes sense, but isn't that easier said than done?"

"Therein lies the problem. Most clients have no idea how to screen potential attorneys. I could claim to be an immigration lawyer, but most people needing an attorney to help with immigration issues wouldn't know if I had extensive experience, little experience, or no experience in that field. You plan on suing a doc?"

I smiled. "No. Curious, that's all."

She took a sip of water, started to say something, when another potential customer entered the store.

"Work calls," she said as she stood.

"I've taken enough of your time. How about grabbing supper tomorrow?"

"Sounds good. Want to meet at Rita's?"

"Perfect. Six?"

She nodded and went to greet the latest arrival, and I grabbed a box of Milk Duds from the plastic pumpkin on the counter.

Chapter Fourteen

One of my favorite activities is taking early morning walks along Center Street. Most of the stores and restaurants are closed, the sidewalks empty. A vehicle occasionally passed as its sleepy driver navigated his or her way to work. The sun heightened the saturation of the brightly painted buildings on the west side of the street. Today, as I often did, I ended my walk on the iconic Folly Beach Fishing Pier where I looked back at the island from the thousand foot long structure over the Atlantic then turned and looked out on the seemingly endless ocean. The peaceful view often put my life and thoughts in perspective. How little everything appears when staring at the great expanse of the Atlantic.

After spending twenty minutes watching seagulls floating on air above the water, a hot cup of coffee from Roasted, the Tides Hotel's coffee shop, was just what the doctor ordered. Yes, I occasionally paid for coffee rather than bumming free cups at Bert's Market. Making my way into the warm coffee shop adorned with Halloween decorations on the counter made me realize how chilly I had gotten while daydreaming on the Pier.

I smiled at Penny, the shop's manager, who looked like she had her hands full with a well dressed middle age couple who appeared upset. I sat at one of two small, round tables in the center of the room to wait for Penny to finish with the only other people in the shop. The couple finally stomped away from the counter and took the remaining table. From the look on their faces, neither Penny nor coffee alleviated their irritation.

I moved to the counter, smiled at Penny who rolled her eyes while nodding at the unhappy couple, ordered, then grabbed a copy of *The Post and Courier*, Charleston's daily newspaper, someone had left on the counter by the window overlooking the ocean. Taking up real estate among the news stories were multiple ads for pop up Halloween stores offering discounts on costumes and candy, various ghost tours, and, of course, area haunted houses. In all my years, I never paid much attention to the October holiday; this year had become a tragic exception.

Penny handed me my coffee, I paid, as I told her to have a good day. She whispered it couldn't get worse. I returned to the table, not five feet from the couple.

The woman wearing a white dress with large colorful flowers on it looked more like she was going to a cocktail party than having coffee at the beach. She pointed her coffee stir stick at the man and said, "Fred, calm down. It's not worth blowing up over such an insignificant issue."

"Insignificant!" the man blurted. "They lost our reservation. That's not the way to run a business. Don't they know they can't treat people like us that way?"

Pretending I couldn't hear their debate that probably

could be heard by people in Wales, I buried my head in the newspaper like I was intrigued by a *Giant Sale* on Halloween candy at Harris Teeter.

"Fred, the manager is resolving the issue as we speak. Besides, you know there's a good chance your receptionist failed to make the reservation."

"Miscommunication, my ass," he said in his grating voice. "Erika, sometimes you're so naive."

The woman looked past the man and saw me studying the newspaper. It was like this was the first she'd noticed me seated five feet away.

"Sir, I'm sorry for the disturbance. Didn't see you there."

"No need to apologize," I said, although I suspected one was due Penny.

"Well, it's not neighborly to display one's dirty laundry in public."

The man with her mumbled something followed by a profanity. With his wavy jet black hair, black sports coat, gold Rolex, and heavy jowls, he reminded me of a Mafioso boss.

I smiled at the lady. "I hope your vacation gets better."

"Thanks, but we're not on vacation. We're moving here next month. Came over from our apartment in Summerville for a couple of days to check the progress on our house. It's being renovated."

"Welcome to the island, I'm Chris Landrum."

"Mr. Landrum, I'm Erika, this handsome man is Fred, my husband."

Fred glared at me like I was interfering with his delightful morning, then said, "Dr. Fred Robinson."

I faked a smile. "Please call me Chris. It's quite a coincidence, but I've been through your house. Great property."

Erika said, "When it was for sale?"

Fred added, "You know I won the bidding war."

Duh! I thought.

"No, Dr. Robinson," I said, with an emphasis on Dr. "A friend and I went through the haunted house."

Erika looked like she'd seen a ghost as she twisted a napkin between her hands before pushing her mid length, black, curly hair out of her face. "Oh."

"Chris, pull up a seat," Dr. Robinson said as he pointed to my chair.

How could I resist since I'd been wondering how I'd meet the house owners?

Fred appeared to have put his foul mood on the back burner as he said, "You were at the haunted house, so you know about the issue we're having."

I didn't think the fate of Todd Lee was Fred's issue, but why not jump in with both feet and see what the owners have to say about *their* issue.

"A friend and I were there when the body was discovered. Not the scare we were looking for."

Erika said, "Fred, what're the chances we'd run into someone who was there when a deceased gentleman was found in our house?" Her face formed a smile that more closely resembled a grimace. "Not the introduction to the community we wanted."

"Did either of you know Todd Lee, the victim?"

After a long pause, Fred cleared his throat and said, "Why would we know some dead guy?"

"What Fred's trying to say is we don't know anybody on the island, so there's no reason to know the victim."

"I only thought that since Mr. Lee was killed in your house, there's a chance you might've known him."

Fred said, "We've not moved in. The house is ours in name only. If I were you, I'd speak to John Rice about the guy. He's doing the renovation and is on site daily, or he's supposed to be. I'm paying good money for the house to be in tip top condition and so far have seen little progress."

I didn't see reason to tell them I'd already talked to Rice. Instead, I said, "Have you visited the house recently?"

Fred said, "Several weeks ago. My dental practice has been keeping me busy. Today is my first trip since then." He turned to Erika, "How do you like the progress so far?" He glanced at me. "My wife is the creative mind behind the renovations."

She said, "I haven't been there in several days, but thought John was making good progress."

"We'll see," Fred added.

"Hope when it's finished, it meets your expectations. It's in a great location and the people on Folly are extremely welcoming."

Erika smiled, seemingly sincere this time. "Thank you, Chris. It'll be nice to finally put down roots."

"You from around here?"

"New Jersey," Fred said. "Moved to Savannah to be a partner in a large dental practice. Opened the office in Charleston."

"Will you be opening an office on the island?"

"No, I'll remain at my practice in Charleston. More money, upscale clientele, you know."

The temperature in the room dropped several degrees with that statement, so I figured my welcome had better come to an end before I told him what I thought of his upscale clientele or their dentist. After all, I didn't want to alienate the charming Dr. Robinson.

"I must be going," I said. "It was a pleasure meeting you. Again, welcome to Folly."

Erika said, "It was nice meeting a local, hope to see you around town."

Dr. Robinson stood and offered his hand. "Pleasure, I'm sure."

Everyone has a right to his opinion.

Chapter Fifteen

I was on the screened in porch finishing my cup of coffee when the sound of a bike coming in the drive broke my peaceful morning.

"Hey, Chris, narrowed down our suspect list?"

"Morning, Charles," I said, wondering if he had a normal greeting in his vocabulary.

"Guess that's no to suspect narrowing. Want to head to the Dog where we can talk about what we know."

I said, "You buying?"

"Penny saved is a penny earned. Your idea, so you buy."

I'd have more luck arguing the facts with a magnolia leaf, so I might as well have a meal and see what my friend has up his long sleeve sweatshirt with what looked like a deranged weasel in a baseball cap staring at me.

I pointed to his shirt. "Nice weasel."

"Weasel, ha! I'll have you know this is the mighty Minnesota Golden Gopher."

"Weasel, gopher same difference."

"Chris, I don't know what to do with you."

Charles started pushing his bike toward the road. That answered how we were traveling to our favorite restaurant. I wasn't sure if the gentleman with the weasel/gopher on his shirt would want to be seen with such an uneducated zoologist, but I took my chances and followed.

The temperature was comfortable, so we accepted a table on the front patio. Amber arrived smiling and shaking her head.

"Haven't seen you two in days. Want the regular or are we going to be adventurous?"

Charles returned her smile. "Surprise me with the usual and whatever His Highness wants."

Amber left with our orders leaving me to be interrogated by Charles.

He said, "I'm not sure we're closer to finding out who killed Todd."

"Nope."

"What're we going to do about it? Shouldn't we be narrowing down suspects instead of adding to the list?"

"First, we should mind our own business. It's not our job. Second, we know near nothing about Todd Lee, so how could we have a list of suspects, that is, if it was our business."

"I agree, it's not our job. This is our passion, something we're good at."

Guess he missed the part about it not being something we should be involved with, regardless if it's a job or a passion.

Amber arrived with our food and asked if there was anything else we needed before heading to the only other occupied table on the patio. We said we were fine.

I took a bite of French toast and started to tell him about yesterday's conversation with the Robinsons when I noticed Shannon Stone heading to the entry. She reminded me of a gypsy in her long, colorful skirt and a flowery blouse. Lugh trotting beside her reminded me of a horse.

She nodded, smiled politely then stuck her head in the door, I assume to request a table on the dog friendly patio. Lugh didn't bother acknowledging me. Shannon and her massive canine walked to the side entrance to the patio where Amber met her and pointed to a large, round table at the front corner.

Before Amber returned to Shannon's table with a bowl of water for Lugh and to take Shannon's order, Charles was petting and carrying on a conversation with his new canine friend.

I took a few steps to their table and said, "Shannon, nice seeing you again and of course you too, Lugh."

I introduced Charles, although Lugh had been Charles's new friend for thirty seconds or so. Charles pulled away from his lovefest, wiped Lugh's slobber off his cheek, then asked Shannon about her dog. No more than three minutes later, we'd learned Lugh was from Ireland, was a present from Shannon's grandmother to remind her of the old country, and is a baby, only a year old. I'm sure there was more, but that's all I remembered.

Shannon looked at our table and at the three empty chairs at her table, before saying, "Would you like to join us."

I said, "Don't want to impose."

As I could've guessed, Charles said, "We'd love to, and Lugh thinks it's a good idea."

Charles grabbed the chair next to Lugh. I got our plates

and drinks from the nearby table and pulled out the seat across from Shannon. This could get interesting quickly, not knowing what Charles might say, or how Shannon would react.

"I don't recall seeing you here before," I said to reenter the conversation.

"Lugh and I come once a week or so after a beach walk. We collect shells. It's our day to enjoy each other's company away from the house."

"Sounds nice," I said.

Shannon turned to Charles, "If I am not being overly forward, Charles, I sense you're wishing to ask me something."

Maybe she could tell fortunes, or at least read minds. I took a deep breath and waited. I'd never known anyone who'd welcomed Charles's interrogation.

Amber noticed we'd moved. She brought us two new drinks, refilled Shannon's and quietly walked away.

Charles whispered something to Lugh before turning to Shannon. "Now that you mention it, I do have a question or two."

"Charles, perhaps we should let Shannon eat in peace."

Shannon smiled. "That's okay, Chris."

Smirking at me, Charles said, "Told you."

I took a sip of coffee and waited.

Charles said, "Do you know about the body in the haunted house?"

"Yes, Roisin told me about it the night it was discovered."

"Did you know him or how he died?"

"I didn't even know it was a male. I do not read the papers and we don't possess a television."

Before Charles bombarded her with questions, I said, "Shannon, the gentleman was Todd Lee. He was stabbed."

Shannon's face paled more than it naturally was. She lowered her head and mumbled something before slowly raising her head, taking a sip of water, while looking at Lugh. The dog sensed her gaze and thumped his tail on the patio floor.

She finally said, "You certain it was Todd?"

I nodded. "You know him?"

"Yes and no. He was passing our house a while back and saw me in the yard weeding. Asked if I needed help."

"That was kind," I said, thinking it didn't sound like the man others had described.

"Todd has, umm, had a damaged soul; the two halves were conflicted. I saw this and thought I could help."

Charles said, "How?"

"Todd assisted with weeding and herb gathering, then he came inside for tea. We talked for a time."

"Interesting," I said. "He tell you anything about his life?"

"Not much. He had a rough time for several years; couldn't find a place he could relax and call home. Unfinished business stalled his progression."

Charles said, "Did he say what the unfinished business was?"

I added, "Shannon, we're trying to figure out why someone would want to harm Todd."

Charles looked at me with an expression that screamed, see, I told you you're trying to catch the killer.

Shannon didn't notice. "I did not ask, simply let him talk. The more he talked the more relaxed and peaceful he seemed, so I didn't want to push him. That's not my way."

"Did Lugh like him?" Charles asked as if it was a logical question.

"Lugh welcomed Todd in the house but did not leave my side. He showed no aggression, or I would not have invited Todd in. One should always rely on their canine companion's instincts."

Lugh, hearing, his name sat and looked Charles eye to eye. Charles rubbed his ears and spoke to him in the language only the two of them understood.

"Sorry we're asking so many questions," I said. "Not many people here knew Todd. You're giving a different perspective. Did you only see him once?"

"A week later, I was in the parlor doing a card reading for a neighbor and glanced outside. Todd was in the garden. When my session was over, I went out to speak to him, but he was gone."

Charles said, "He didn't stick around to talk?"

"He was gone but had picked sage and left it on the steps along with an amethyst."

I said, "Are those significant?"

"Yes, amethyst calms fears, allows peaceful dreams and spiritual growth to name a few. Sage is used to cleanse, to banish negative energy. It can also be used to give strength."

"Why would he leave them for you?"

"I took it as a sign he was preparing to face whatever was bothering him and to make a new start." She looked at her watch. "Sorry, but we need to head to the house."

I said, "We enjoyed the chance to talk."

As Shannon stood to leave, she said, "One last thing, I gave Todd my husband's business card in case what was disturbing his life required a lawyer."

"Did they ever talk?"

"I don't know."

After they were gone, Charles said, "We now have more answers."

"A few, but way more questions, Mr. Detective."

I started to tell him about talking with the Robinson's when we arrived, but Shannon's visit stopped me. Time to get it over.

"Guess who I had coffee with yesterday morning?"

Charles was usually the one who asked questions I couldn't possibly know the answers to. It felt good being on the asking end.

"Wasn't me."

"That your best guess?"

"That's not a guess, it's a fact."

"Erika and Dr. Fred Robinson."

He glared at me. "And when were you going to tell me?"

"When we got here, then Shannon arrived."

"How many hours was that after you had coffee with the Robinson's yesterday morning?" He stuck out his lower lip.

"Want me to do math or tell you what we talked about?"

He sighed. "What did you talk about?"

I told him about the strange conversation, my negative reaction to Dr. Robinson, and the cheerful dentist telling me to talk to John Rice if I wanted to know about the body.

"Chris, you think he killed Todd Lee?"

"What could be his motive?"

"Nary a clue. How about obnoxious people do obnoxious things? Killing Lee would qualify."

"You'll need to do better than that."

"Okay, how about … umm, no, wait, how about … I'll go back to nary a clue. Why do you think?"

"Charles, to quote a friend, I have *nary a clue*."

Chapter Sixteen

I was on the way home with a TV dinner from Bert's, when Officer Spencer pulled in the lot between my cottage and the store.

Allen stepped out of the cruiser, chuckled, then said, "Been to more haunted houses?"

I didn't share his glee. "Don't remind me."

"Heard the latest?"

Another impossible question to answer.

I shrugged.

"Sheriff's Office made an arrest in the haunted house murder."

"Who?"

"Don't know his name, some homeless guy."

"How'd they catch him?"

"You know as much about it as I do. Heard it this afternoon." He looked toward Bert's door. "Gotta grab something to eat then back to work. Good seeing you."

I told him the feeling was mutual before heading home to stick supper in the microwave.

As I ate my "home cooked" meal, my mind drifted to what Allen had shared. He might not know anything else about the arrest, but I knew someone who would.

"Cindy, did I catch you at a bad time?"

"In fact, Mr. Pest, you did. Dear, sweet hubby and I were sitting down to an exquisitely prepared, sumptuous meal of hot dogs, slathered with the good mustard, not that cheap yellow stuff, and Pringles. Can I fix a gourmet meal or what?"

I held back a laugh then told her I was sorry to interrupt their meal and asked her to call me while it was being digested. She mumbled a response through a mouthful of her gourmet meal before hanging up. I assumed she'd been saying she'd be thrilled to call me back.

She returned the call an hour later with, "Thought I'd call while Larry was watching *Wheel of Fortune*. He goes ballistic if I disturb him during *Wheel*. The little perv claims the show stimulates his mind, but if you ask me, he's watching Vanna White. Don't ask what she stimulates. Woe, that's way more than you need to know. What do you want?"

"This afternoon I heard the Sheriff's Office made an arrest in Todd Lee's murder."

"Yep," she said before the phone went dead.

I called her back.

Cindy answered, "Vanna White fan club."

I smiled. "Tell me about the murder suspect."

She sighed. "Name's Jeff Hildebrand, mid thirties, homeless until yesterday when he was given a luxury cell in the Charleston County Cannon Detention Center."

"What led them to him?"

"Beverly Kosfeld."

"The elderly lady who rides around town on an adult trike?"

"Chris, yes, if you mean an oversized tricycle like you geezers ride."

"How'd she lead you to him?"

"She shuffled in my office day before yesterday saying she just heard someone got killed in the haunted house. She lives in the Oceanfront Villas, in a unit directly across the street from the murder site."

"Didn't she hear or see all the commotion the night the body was found?"

"Excellent question, fledgling detective. Sweet Beverly hears about as good as a squid, which in case you're interested, can't hear at all. She, Beverly, not the squid, has come close to getting herself squashed by a car more than once because she couldn't hear them coming. She—"

"Got it. She didn't hear anything."

"You want to know what happened or not?"

"Cindy, of—"

She interrupted, "After she learned of the murder, she remembered seeing Todd Lee going into the house late at night after everything was shut down. She didn't think anything of it; figured he worked on the crew getting the house ready for its haunting or worked in it after it closed."

"How'd she know it was Todd Lee?"

"She nearly ran into him with her tricycle a week earlier, slammed on the brakes, then began apologizing. She told him who she was, he told her who he was. That's how. Follow me so far?"

"Yes, so how'd she know who the Hildebrand guy was, and why'd she think he killed Todd?"

"Said she saw some guy going in the house with Todd two or three times. She didn't know who he was. Apparently, she didn't almost run him down to get his name."

"How'd you all identify him?"

"Beverly sees better than she hears. She described him, down to the black Lynyrd Skynyrd sweatshirt he was wearing. I asked around and Officer Bishop remembered seeing someone with that description hanging around the Folly River Park a couple of nights earlier. We found him later that day and turned him over to Detective Adair. The rest is history."

"Don't suppose he confessed."

"You don't suppose correctly. While he didn't solve the murder, he did solve one mystery."

"That being?"

"Where Todd Lee hung his hat several nights. That is, if he had a hat. According to suspect Jeff, he and Todd stayed nights in the haunted house. When Todd worked for the renovation company, he made a key to the house; then on colder nights, he went in after hours to crash. After Todd was fired, he couldn't afford a place to stay and ran into Jeff Hildebrand on the street."

"Cindy, I didn't see anything, but did the detectives or their techs find evidence Todd was staying in the haunted house?"

"Another excellent question. This is where it gets interesting. Hildebrand claims he came to the haunted house about two o'clock the day the body was found. Said he had a lead on where he and Todd could get a cheap room. He thought if they combined their worldly resources, they might be able to scrape up enough to pay rent." Cindy hesitated before saying, "Yes, Larry. I'll fix popcorn when I get off the phone. Umm, sorry about that Chris, my wifely duties are never done. Where was I?"

"Hildebrand came to find Todd."

"Oh yeah, he found him all right, but claims Todd was dead when he got there. Says he panicked, grabbed everything there belonging to him and Todd, and skedaddled."

"Don't suppose Detective Adair believed him."

"Not for a second, but the problem is that pesky thing called proof. He ain't got none."

"Is Jeff still in jail?"

"Currently charged with evidence tampering. Won't have to prove that since he confessed to it. That's a misdemeanor, so if convicted Hildebrand could get up to a year at taxpayer expense. That may give Adair time to find more evidence. Or so he hopes."

"Why may?"

"Adair says even the greenest public defender could get Hildebrand out on bail since evidence tampering, especially in this case, isn't serious enough to hold him until trial."

"Does Hildebrand have bail money?"

"He could. Adair said it wouldn't take much."

"Think he killed Lee?"

"Beats Blackbeard or Chucky doing it."

Chapter Seventeen

October gifted Folly Beach with another mild morning. Not wanting to be cooped up in the house, I grabbed my windbreaker in case my walk took me to the beach, then grabbed a cup of coffee at Bert's. Among the many nice things about the off season is the lack of vacationers which makes walks serene and less crowded, especially along Center Street. With all the twists and turns I've experienced through the last decade, Folly feels more like my hometown than where I grew up in Kentucky. The island has offered me a fantastic although eccentric group of friends and interesting adventures. As I walked, I realized how lucky I was to have landed in this community.

"Brother Chris!" A booming voice broke the morning air like thunder as I passed Center Street Coffee. I hadn't noticed Preacher Burl sitting at a small table at the side of the small shop.

"Preacher Burl, sorry I didn't see you."

"It's no wonder, you looked like you were in never never

land." He laughed. "I've been told I get that look when I'm working on sermons."

"I was daydreaming, not sermon writing."

"Brother Chris, I bet you'd have no trouble writing a good sermon."

"Preacher, Lugh would have a better chance writing a novel than I would penning a sermon. I'll leave the words of wisdom and hope to you. Enjoying the weather?"

"I just left young Roisin after one of our nature walks. That young lady is going to make sure I recognize all the fauna and flora on the island."

"One of us has to learn it since I apparently don't know the difference between a weasel and a gopher."

"Meaning?"

"It's a Charles thing," I said, knowing that'd be all I needed to say since Burl knew most of Charles's quirks. "How's Roisin?"

"She's good, excited her dad's taking time off the next couple of weeks to get ready for All Hallows Eve, Halloween to you and me."

"Didn't realize there was that much to do for Halloween."

Clearing his throat while putting on his best teaching face, Burl said, "According to Roisin, Halloween or All Hallows Eve, Samhain is one of their most important Sabbats."

"Preacher, that's a couple of words I'm not familiar with."

"Brother Chris, me too. I'm spouting off what I learned today, hoping it'll help me remember some of it better."

"Humm, okay, enlighten me."

"Wicca celebrates eight different holidays they call

Sabbats, and Samhain is another name for what Christians refer to as Halloween."

I thought how only a few days ago I was blissfully ignorant of this unique way of life. I was equally surprised how a preacher of the Christian faith was so embracing of a religion that seemed so different.

Burl smiled, "Enough learning for today unless you want to acquire knowledge about the Carolina anole."

Finally, something I knew about.

"No, I'm good," I said, thinking how those little lizards have a party on my porch daily. They're some of God's little critters you get used to in the Carolinas. They're everywhere. Fortunately, they eat ants which are unwelcomed visitors in any cottage.

"Lesson over, but I'm glad I ran into you. There is something else regarding the Stones."

"What?"

Burl looked around to see if anyone was near, which I thought strange since the road was void of life except a black and white cat walking up the middle of the street like he owned it.

"Brother Mike called this morning to let me know Roisin was running late. He also asked if I would be comfortable setting up a meeting with us. Was going to call you when I got home."

"Us, like you and me?"

"Yes."

"Why?"

"Not sure, but he thought it best I invite you instead of approaching you directly since you'd never met. Are you willing?"

"Sure, when?"

Burl looked at his watch, then said, "This afternoon, if you're not too busy."

I wondered if Burl knew how not busy I was most days?

"That'll work. He in a hurry?"

"I wouldn't say urgent, but something in the way he asked made me think it'd be better sooner rather than later."

"What time and where?" I asked, hoping not at Mike's house. I was in no hurry to see Lugh or Ozzy, aka Desmond.

"I'll check with Brother Mike to nail down the time but let's say one o'clock unless that won't work for him. We can meet at First Light." He smiled. "I'll even provide lunch."

I cut my short walk shorter and headed home wondering why Mike Stone wanted to meet. Then again, how bad could it be since I was getting a free lunch. It'd be a pleasant change since I normally got stuck with the check. The black and white cat escorted me most of the way home. I was ready to tell him he wouldn't find Friskies at my house when he trotted past me without a backward glance, then ran behind Bert's.

I spent the next two hours flipping through photo magazines and wondering what Mike Stone could want. I also must've fallen asleep since the next thing I remembered was the clock revealing I had twenty minutes to get to the meeting.

Most First Lights' services are held on the beach near the Folly Pier. The location of today's meeting was in a building that was used as a foul weather sanctuary and a base for Preacher Burl to meet with individuals or small groups from his congregation, or as he refers to them, his flock. The building isn't what most people think of when visualizing a church. It's next to Barb's Books and faces

Center Street. It has no stained glass windows or a steeple, but more important than those physical features, it has a dedicated flock and a caring minister.

A block before I got to the First Light, I noticed a man exiting a turquoise 1965 Mustang Fastback in front of the church then entering the sanctuary. I used my detective skills and deduced it was the person I was to meet. I walked in and was greeted by the aroma of hamburgers. Over the years, I've learned most kids love hamburgers, then as they grow up, the love changes to a simply they're okay. When people reach their second childhood, the love of burgers returns. Okay, by most kids, I'm referring to yours truly.

"Brother Chris, glad you could make it," Burl said as we shook hands. It struck me as odd since the preacher is always polite, but seldom shook hands. I wondered if this was his way of showing I was no threat to the witch, or was it warlock?

I finally got a better look at Mike Stone who'd been standing behind Burl. The newcomer was slightly taller than me and perhaps twenty pounds heavier. He was wearing a red polo shirt and jeans. Clearly, Desmond didn't get his fashion style from his dad.

"Glad to be here; you must be Mr. Stone," I said.

We shook hands. He gave me what appeared to be a sincere smile that seemed nothing like the one given by some lawyers I've met.

"I'm only Mr. Stone in court; please call me Mike."

Burl led us to a table across the room before saying, "Let's sit, break bread, and have a pleasant conversation."

Silence filled the room as we each grabbed a burger and an iced tea. Burl joked that the food came from the Crab

Shack and not his kitchen, so we wouldn't have to fear food poisoning.

After a few bites, and an uncomfortable silence, Mike said, "Chris, I guess you're curious why I wanted to meet."

"I admit, I was surprised when Burl mentioned it."

Mike smiled. "You've become a topic of conversation at my house."

I find it strange anyone would be sitting around the house talking about me.

"Why? I'm not that interesting."

Mike continued to smile. "Oh, but you are. Roisin thinks you are a nice man who is open to new ideas."

"I've always been a good listener. Your daughter is brighter than some adults I know."

"Roisin is an old soul, not her first go around." The smile across Mike's face was beyond a proud dad, more akin to pure admiration. "Shannon tells me your aura is peaceful and shows you're trustworthy. Not a common reading nowadays."

I glanced over at Burl to see his take. No reaction.

"I'm not sure what to say."

"I understand. Trust me, I'm normally not forthcoming with our personal beliefs. Were you reared on Folly?"

"No, I'm a transplant from Kentucky."

"I'm sure Shannon told you, we moved from Minnesota where I attended University of Minnesota Law School. That's where I found the love of my life and earned a law degree."

"Was Shannon in law school with you?"

Mike's warm laugh made me feel like I was one of his best friends. "Sorry, what's funny is she hated my career choice. Said it'd be the last degree she'd ever want. Hers is in agricultural. Apparently, she didn't find me as untowardly as my career choice. We met and were married thirty-seven days later."

Burl wagging a fry at the attorney. "Brother Mike, I had no idea you were so impetuous."

"I'm not, simply couldn't see my life without her by my side. One might say our stars aligned."

I said, "You're a lucky man."

With the meal a few bites from finished, I was certain the reason for the meeting hadn't come up, that is unless Mike was curious about my aura.

"Very lucky. Chris, shall I get to why I asked Burl to get us together?"

I nodded.

"Shannon told me you were asking about Todd Lee."

"Did you know him?"

"I talked to Mr. Lee twice, once by phone then at Loggerhead."

"Do you mind if I ask what you talked about?"

"Chris, not sure you know, attorney client privilege remains even after death."

I nodded. "Todd was a client?"

"Not a paying client, but yes, he told me what was on his mind and I gave him advice with regards to the law. Technically, he didn't hire me, simply needed someone to listen to. Doing that, I could also provide legal advice if he needed it."

"Don't mean to pry but did it seem he was going to take your advice?"

Of course, I was prying. Charles wasn't here so how else would I get answers?

Mike stared at me, briefly glancing at Burl while rubbing

the back of his neck. "With him ending up dead, I'm guessing he didn't take my advice. Not surprising, Todd didn't strike me as being genuinely nice."

"Shannon told me he was troubled. Did you get a different impression?"

"Let's just say after our meeting at Loggerheads, Mr. Lee knew I didn't want him at my house." He hesitated before saying, "Chris, I wanted to let you know I knew Mr. Lee, that he appeared more than troubled, and was no longer welcome at my house. I can't tell you more."

"Have you talked to the police?"

"Not yet."

"I don't know the Sheriff's Office detective that well but know Cindy LaMond, Folly's Chief. If you know anything you can share that could help them find his killer, I'd suggest you talk with her."

"I'll take that under advisement."

Since Todd wasn't technically a client, I didn't see why Mike couldn't tell Cindy, but I didn't get the impression I'd convinced him.

We spent the next fifteen minutes talking about the weather, restaurants along Center Street, Folly's proximity to Charleston, and other things strangers discuss. Sensing our discussion nearing an end, instead of pushing him about Todd Lee, I said, "Mike, it's been a pleasure meeting you, and Preacher, your company is always welcomed."

Burl said, "Brother Chris, will I see you Sunday?" Burl's smile showed he already knew the answer.

At best, I was an irregular attendee at First Light.

"I'll see."

As Mike and I walked out into the brisk October air, I

couldn't shake the feeling there was something he wanted to tell me away from Burl.

To keep the conversation going, I said, "That's one nice ride, Mike. You don't see many classic Mustangs over here."

"My dad bought her off the showroom floor. Everything's original. She's been taken care of better than most children."

"Is she your daily drive or just for special occasions?"

"If you see me, Banshee will be close by."

"Banshee?"

"Dad named the car, so who am I to change it? I want to extend an open invitation to the Stone house anytime you would like."

"I appreciate that."

I watched Mike open the driver's door, then hesitate as if he wanted to say more. Other than, "See you later," no words came. As the car pulled from the curb I was left wondering if I just read more into peoples' actions, thanks to Charles noisy influence, or was it something else.

Chapter Eighteen

Over the last few years, I've been trying to lose weight and get in better shape. I've failed miserably, but that hasn't stopped me from telling myself I was trying. Experience has taught me that walking through soft sand on the beach is more strenuous than on paved surfaces. Other than a better cardio exercise, walking along the ocean does much for my spirit, the earlier in the day the better.

Today I headed to the beach, then turned toward the sun wishing me a good morning as it peeked its head over the Atlantic. The temperature was already in the upper sixties, high for this close to Halloween. The only life I noticed was a colony of seagulls searching for breakfast at water's edge.

I don't know what I'd been thinking, but it must've been time consuming. I looked up and saw I'd already walked nine blocks from Center Street. I also was oblivious to the thick fog rolling in off the ocean. Before I became oblivious to walking into the surf and drowning, I turned and headed back toward the center of town. Fortunately, I had the coastline to guide me toward the Pier since the view in front of me was of nothing but thick, gray fog.

It was a couple more blocks before I saw life other than seagulls. The vague image of two people walking toward me came into focus, almost focus. Fifty yards closer, I recognized the images as Roisin and Desmond Stone. Roisin wore a long skirt, bright red blouse, a backpack, and was barefoot. Her brother had on black jeans, cuffs rolled up, a black T shirt with Black Flag plastered across the front, and black, hiking boots.

Roisin said. "Hi, Mr. Chris, out for a walk?"

While I thought it was obvious, I said, "Yes. Good morning, Roisin, Desmond." She smiled; Desmond looked at me like he'd seen a sea monster. "Going somewhere in particular?"

Roisin's smile increased. "Enjoying Mother Nature's glorious gifts." She chuckled. "That is until she dumped fog on us."

"Sea fog," Desmond said. His sour look unchanged.

"What's Black Flag?" I asked to offer something he might want to talk about."

"Punk rock band," He shook his head and said, as if who wouldn't know that.

Clearly, I didn't. "Oh."

Roisin twisted her feet in the soft sand and said, "That's okay, Mr. Chris, I didn't know it until my punk rock brother told me fifteen times."

I saw why Preacher Burl thought so highly of the young lady.

Desmond sneered at his sister before turning to me. "Sea fog. Stories about it have been around for centuries. Ghost ships, boats disappearing in it never to be seen again. Sea monsters grabbing crew members right off the deck during outbreaks of the fog."

"Mr. Chris," Roisin said, "you don't have to pay attention to him. His brain works different than yours or mine."

What to say to that?

I didn't have to say anything. Desmond said, "You've heard of the Bermuda Triangle, haven't you?"

"Sure."

He pointed toward the ocean. "It's nearby, right out there. Countless ships floated into it; many never came out. Airplanes flew into it; bunches of them were never seen again."

Roisin kicked sand at her brother, then rolled her eyes. "How many times do I have to tell you the Bermuda Triangle is nowhere near Folly Beach. It's down south."

"Like you know everything," Desmond said. "Bermuda is right out there, and the triangle goes from it down to Puerto Rico then to Florida. Look it up." He turned to me, "Not all the mysteries of the sea happen out there." He pointed to the ocean. "Mister, see how the sea fog also covers land?"

I nodded; Roisin rolled her eyes again; and Desmond pointed toward town, before saying, "Bad stuff happens there." He stared at me; his eyes narrowed. "You're the guy that saw the stiff in the haunted house. Cool."

"Desmond," Roisin said, "nothing's cool about it. The man was killed."

Desmond ignored his sister. "Me and little squirt here went through the haunted house the night after the dead guy was found. That preacher man was going to take her the night before, but death killed that plan." He rolled his eyes. "Anyway, we had to get there early because so many people wanted to see where the dead guy was." He laughed, an emotion I hadn't seen from him. "Scared the crap out of sissy here." He nodded toward Roisin.

"You were scared too when that clown sat up in the coffin."

"Wasn't," Desmond said before turning to me. "You hear about the broom some bozo left on our porch?"

I thought Charles could change directions on the head of a pin. He could learn from Desmond.

"I heard it somewhere. Why?"

"Wondering. Some people think we're weird."

Roisin said, "Everyone thinks you're weird."

"Sis, you know I meant because we're witches."

"Wiccans," she said.

"No difference to the ignorant," Desmond said. "Stupid people think all of us fly around on brooms. Everybody knows brooms can't fly." He nodded his head slowly then said, "Chris, if I may call you that, we're modern witches. I fly on a Eureka Mighty Mite vacuum cleaner. Some witches prefer Bissell, but the Mighty Mite has more power."

Roisin said, "Mr. Chris, you have to overlook things my brother says. Most of his fog's in his head. His brains were sucked out long ago, probably by a Bissell vacuum cleaner."

I thought her comment was humorous but didn't want to upset Desmond. "I'll keep that in mind, Roisin."

"Mr. Chris, Dad said he met you yesterday."

"Yes, we had a nice talk. He's a nice—"

Desmond interrupted, "He tell you he knew the stiff?"

Roisin shoved her brother. "Mr. Chris, we need to get home. Mom worries when I'm out too long with Desmond.

She's afraid he'll be a bad influence." She leaned close to me and whispered, "Mom's a smart lady."

That I could see. I could also see how the conversation about the late Todd Lee was over. "Nice talking to both of you."

Roisin said she looked forward to it. Desmond wasn't that positive, but did say, "Remember, I'll be the one flying the Mighty Mite."

"How could I forget?"

They headed to the dunes line and I continued toward the Folly Pier.

The fog was lifting so I was less afraid of disappearing, being confronted by a sea monster, or buzzed by a vacuum cleaner riding witch.

Chapter Nineteen

Thoughts of Todd Lee swirled in my head all morning, so I decided I needed to think about something else. Food seemed like a good option. I hadn't been to Loggerhead's in a couple of weeks, so it fit the bill. Mother Nature was still blessing us with warm weather making it another day to give my car a break and to motivate my exercise rationale. I was a block away when I realized the real reason I was headed to Loggerhead's wasn't only the food, but where it was located. Dr. Robinson's house, aka the last haunted house I hoped I'd ever attend, was adjacent to the popular restaurant. I wanted to see what if anything was happening there. The haunted house didn't look too haunted in daylight or it might've been all the activity going on around it. Construction trucks filled the driveway and workers were everywhere. I spotted Nate Davis lugging a sheet of drywall up the front stairs.

I waited for him to set the heavy load on the landing, then said, "Nate, what's going on?"

He looked around before spotting me at the bottom of the stairs. "Hey Chris, come to help?"

I assumed, hoped, he was joking. "You working upstairs? What about the haunted house?"

"It's history."

"Meaning?"

"Dr. Pain In The Ass shut it down."

"What happened?"

He shrugged. "Boss man's out back; he has the answers. I need to get back to work. Maybe I'll catch you at Cal's."

I watched him maneuver the drywall through the front door, then headed around back. The first thing to catch my attention was a petite woman with a blond ponytail wearing a pink hard hat operating a table saw. With my faux detective mind in gear, I deduced she was the B of J&B. I stopped ten feet in front of the action so I wouldn't startle her and cause an OSHA investigation.

She switched off the saw, removing her ear protection, and bounced over to greet me. She reminded me of a cocker spaniel puppy, full of energy and cheer while doing more manual labor than I've ever done.

She said, "What can I do for you?"

"Sorry to interrupt. I was looking for John?"

"Oh lord, what's my husband done now?" Instead of waiting for me to tell her what her husband had done, she turned and surveyed the backyard until she spotted her target. "He's leaning against that tree looking important. I figure he's thinking about lunch."

"Thank you."

As I walked over, I heard the saw start up and what I thought was singing but wasn't sure.

John spotted me.

I said, "You look like a busy man."

"Chris, what a surprise. Busy, no just thinking about lunch."

"A man after my own heart. I was on my way to Loggerhead's when I saw Nate hauling drywall upstairs."

"Yeah it sucks." He shook his head. "Dr. Robinson."

"That's what Nate said. He told me you were the man with the depressing details."

"Sure am, but since you were on your way to lunch and I need a break, why don't we make it a luncheon pow wow."

"Sounds good."

John pushed away from the tree, set his hard hat on an overturned bucket, walked to the table saw where I'd previously stood, and tapped his watch.

The woman ignored John, turned to me, and said, "Told you he was thinking about lunch."

John said, "You two know each other?"

"Yes," she said, "known each other two whole minutes. He was looking for you, so I told him whatever you did illegal, I didn't know anything about it. I added where to find you."

"Sounds like something you'd do," John said, then turned to me. "Chris, I'd like to introduce my lovely, crazy wife Bri."

"Pleasure to meet you, Bri."

"You as well," she said then tapped John on the arm. "So boss, where are you taking our new friend and your lovely, not crazy, wife to lunch?"

"Going to a land far away." He nodded toward Loggerhead's.

Bri chuckled and turned to me. "You'll learn to take what you can get from this big bear." She pointed her hard hat at John. "Shall we walk or should I expect a limo."

"You wait for the limo. Chris and I'll walk."

Bri set her hard hat, gloves, and ear protection on the saw table and in one quick motion, pulled off her long sleeve, plaid shirt revealing a pink tank top. She locked arms with John as we headed to lunch.

It took no more than a minute to make the limo less trip to Loggerhead's then up the stairs to the entry. John asked the hostess for a table on the deck overlooking the former haunted house. It was a good choice considering a warm, late October day couldn't be taken for granted. Decorations were still hanging from every vertical surface from the restaurant's annual Halloween Costume Party held last evening. Since Costume was in the event's name, I wasn't in attendance. I also wasn't qualified for the restaurant's Halloween Pet Costume Party that was advertised on as poster by the door.

We were one of three occupied tables, so a server was quick to arrive, told us she was Doris, and asked what we wanted to drink. We each requested iced tea.

Doris headed inside and I said, "Bri, you've chosen a career most women wouldn't consider."

"That's what my parents said when I left home."

John leaned my direction. "Bri is one of the best construction workers I've worked with, stronger than many of the guys." He laughed. "That's even if she needs a ladder to reach the truck bed."

"Funny," Bri said. "That's why I married a man the size of an oak."

"I'm only six-five, but to a woman who's shorter than a hobbit, well, you get the picture."

I was at a loss for a response, but fortunately I didn't need one. Doris returned with our drinks and asked if we were ready to order. John and Bri went with cheeseburgers. To not slow things down, I said the same.

John watched Doris leave then said, "Chris, you had questions about the haunted house closing?"

"What happened? I heard it was bringing in good crowds."

"Not good, great. Was the best venture we've done. All the proceeds were going to charity and the locals loved the entertainment." He shook his head. "A huge loss all around."

"Damned shame," Bri added.

I said, "So why close?"

John took a sip, slammed his plastic glass on the table, and said, "Dr. Robinson blew a gasket with the large crowds and a lack of progress on the renovation."

Bri said, "John assured him we were on schedule and described the benefits of keeping the haunted house open."

I said, "It didn't matter?"

"Do you know the good doctor?"

"Had the pleasure of meeting him once. A real charmer."

"Don't know the half of it," John said. "In my business, I deal with lots of different people and some are difficult, but none as disagreeable as Fred."

Bri put her hand on John's shoulder. "Boss man tried to convince Doctor-Feel-No-Good, but the jerk wouldn't budge even with the offer of another discount."

"That didn't sway him?'

John said, "It ticked him off more."

"Interesting."

"He was fixated on people calling his house the murder house, ruining his good name, he claimed. Wanted the murder forgotten."

"I talked to his wife," Bri said. "Thought a woman to woman conversation would help and to remind her all donations would be in their name. That's what the community would remember."

"Her reaction?"

"Not good, really not good."

"What'd she say?"

"The look that crossed her face, made me take a step back. She proceeded to tell me how her husband owned us, and we needed to do what he said. She said a lot more, but I'm too much of a lady to repeat it."

"Seems strange she got so upset," I said as Doris slid our plates in front of each of us.

"Bri told me the full conversation when we got home. Was smart on her part. No way will I have anyone talking to my wife like that. Furthermore, no one owns me."

"I understand."

"We were grateful for them allowing us to host a haunted house. We didn't want to bring any negativity. The customer is always right, but it was disappointing for all involved."

"The community will miss the entertainment, but at least they had it a couple of weeks."

I took a bite of burger, glanced at the former haunted house, and said, "Bri, what was your impression of Todd Lee?"

"That's a strange question."

"Honey, I've heard Chris is trying to put the cops out of business."

Not the direction I wanted the conversation to head. "Nope, simply curious."

Bri smiled but it quickly faded. "Didn't like him. He was an arrogant know-it-all who thought women should be barefoot and pregnant with no place in a man's world."

I said, "I've heard some things about him but that's new."

She continued, "Met him a year ago in Charleston on a jobsite. He came around asking for work, but John was offsite. He was rude, crude, and made a pass at me. Not the best way to get a job, if you ask me."

John's head pivoted toward Bri. "I had no idea he was that guy. You never told me his name. Bri was out of town when I hired him over here."

Bri tightened the grip on her drink. "Was my first day onsite in a week or so. I was bringing in props for the haunted house and ran into him. Was shocked to see him again. The jerk grabbed my arms and made a comment, one I don't feel comfortable saying in public."

I said, "What happened?"

"Nate walked in the room, saw what Todd was doing, yelled at him. I left to find John."

"I fired him and escorted him off property. End of story."

And it was. The rest of the lunch was filled with talk about their favorite vacation spots and how good the food was. John noted workers had arrived back on site, so he said they'd better get back to work. They paid the tab, including mine, before heading next door.

Leaving Loggerheads, I had more questions than answers about J&B. The story they shared differed from what John had told me earlier about firing Todd.

Chapter Twenty

I waited until mid morning before calling Charles, not because I was afraid if I called earlier, I'd wake him, but I wanted to finish breakfast and coffee before being subjected to his version of the Spanish Inquisition. The weather was more appropriate for this time of year with a light chilly rain enveloping the area. Spending the day inside discussing motives for a haunted house homicide seemed fitting. I took a deep breath and made the call.

"Morning, Charles."

"Who's this? It couldn't be my long lost friend, Chris, could it?"

"Funny, how're you doing?"

"Well, you'd know if you'd bothered to call in the last two months."

"Months? How about the last few days? You suffering a memory lapse?"

"Nope, neglect."

"You know that thing you're talking on can make calls, don't you?"

"Picky, picky. You're the neglector."

I was jumping down a rabbit hole, so I changed the subject. Not fast enough.

He said, "Catch the killer?"

"You know I can't do that without you."

"Precisely."

"Charles, if you're done griping, I thought you might wonder why I called."

"Calling because you're feeling guilty about not calling for two months."

"Charles."

"Okay, why are you calling?"

"Better. To see if you'd like to come over to talk about the murder."

He was gone. I was certain the weather had nothing to do with the silence or the lack of phone etiquette from my neglected friend. I smiled, refilled my coffee mug, then waited on the porch for my guest whom I hadn't seen in somewhere between two days and two months.

Three sips later, Charles was pedaling wildly down the rain soaked streets looking like Almira Gulch in *The Wizard of Oz*.

He jumped off the bike, stepped on the porch, shook water off his Tilley and off the shoulders of his blue and gray, University of New Hampshire long sleeve sweatshirt with a snarling wildcat on the front, then said, "Couldn't you have picked a nicer day?"

"Thought we needed some old fashioned October weather, hence the reason I ordered rain."

"Didn't know you could do that?"

"You don't know everything about me. Iced tea, water, coffee, or Diet Coke?"

"Don't put yourself out," he said as he headed to the kitchen.

I sat in the living room and waited for him to return with his drink of choice. Apparently, today it was iced tea since he was taking a large gulp from a bottle of tea as he flopped down in the chair across from me.

"Enough of the pleasantries," he said. "Let's get started."

"Where do you want to begin?"

"At the beginning, Chris, at the beginning."

"Todd Lee."

"What do we know about the late Mr. Lee?" He leaned in waiting for my revelations.

"He was relatively new to Folly, homeless for the most part. He wasn't liked by most we know who knew him. Also, remember how your new friend Nate Davis told us how Lee kept bragging about striking it rich?"

"A dream of many homeless folks. How many actually find a pot of gold at the end of a rainbow?"

"Zero," I said. "If he kept saying it, he must've had something in mind."

"Like robbing a bank or winning the lottery?"

I shrugged. "Don't know."

"But who'd want to kill him?"

"Could be someone he was scheming with or somebody he was going to get the money from. Who knows?"

Charles mirrored my shrug and said, "Not me."

Since he didn't bring me anything from the kitchen, I left to refill my mug. Truth be told, it was more to delay the grief I would receive from what I was going to share next.

I returned to my chair before saying, "Yesterday I talked to John and Bri."

He leaned forward nearly knocking his bottle of tea off the arm of the chair. "Without me?"

"Wasn't planned, ran into them."

"Where?"

"The haunted house, well, former haunted house."

"Wow, just happened to run into them at the house where you knew they'd be working. What a surprise." He hesitated, tilted his head, and said, "Former haunted house?"

"Dr. Robinson shut it down."

"You're kidding."

"Afraid not."

"That's just not right for the youngsters." He shook his head. "Not right."

"John and Bri were upset."

"I understand. There aren't that many Halloween activities here for the kids. No trick or treat, now no haunted house. You have to admit it was fun before the corpse showed up."

Don't recall ever thinking *really wish we could've finished this fun filled adventure of getting the stuffing scared out of us, instead of staring at a dead body, a real one.* Charles was looking at me waiting for agreement, but I refused.

I said, "I learned Bri had a past with Todd, not a good one."

"Not good?"

I shared what John and Bri had told me about Todd.

"Don't you find that strange since it wasn't mentioned in other conversations with John?" Charles took a drink.

"Yep."

"Now we're getting somewhere. She can be number one on the suspect list."

"Charles, having a past with someone doesn't mean she killed him."

His fingers tapped on the armrest. "I know, but it doesn't hurt."

"Moving on, let's get back to Nate Davis since he didn't like Todd."

Without coming to any insightful conclusions, we discussed Nate's relationship with Todd.

Charles smiled. "Dude told me a homeless man's been arrested for something about the incident."

"Dude? Didn't realize he was part of your detective agency." I didn't add *using the term detective agency loosely*.

"Nope, but he knows the homeless man. His name—"

I interrupted, "Jeff Hillebrand."

"How'd you know?"

"Cindy told me."

He glared at me. "When were you going to tell me?"

"Now."

He sighed then said, "Police think he did it?"

"Yes, but they have no proof. What's Dude's take?"

"Hillebrand's a guy down on his luck with a temper."

"Seems to be a theme."

"Hillebrand could've killed him, but why?" Charles scratched his head in what I translated as either deep concentration or head lice.

"Cindy said he and Todd spent some nights in the haunted house, but because you share a space with someone doesn't mean you have a reason to kill him. From what we've learned, they had tempers." It was my turn to scratch my head wondering how to find out more about Hillebrand.

Charles stood and headed to the kitchen. Since he still had tea in the bottle, I had a hunch I knew what he was looking for; something he wouldn't find since I hadn't been to Harris Teeter recently on one of my rare grocery shopping adventures.

He returned empty handed. "No chips. Really? You expect me to use my brain power without nourishment?"

"Didn't know your brain needed chips to function. That explains a lot," I said, smiling at my friend standing in the doorway looking unamused.

He shook his head. "I'll be back."

Charles grabbed his Tilley and walked out the door before I responded. I took the alone time figuring how I was going to tell my brain starved friend about the other conversations I've had without him. Hopefully, whatever he gets will sooth his bruised ego.

He returned with two bags filled with goodies. I was glad I didn't have a tab at Bert's, or it would've increased from Charles's brain food purchase.

"You're a crappy host, so I brought refreshments to get us through," he said as he headed to the kitchen.

"Kind of you. When you're done in there, I'll tell you who else I've talked with."

He returned to the living room carrying chips and salsa and said, "More secret meetings?"

"Charles, they weren't secret anything," I said looking at his sad puppy dog face.

"Then, non secret meetings with?"

"Mike Stone, Shannon's husband."

"Lugh's dad?"

"You could say that. Mike knew Todd. Spoke with him twice."

That stopped Charles mid chew. "What'd he say?"

"Mike talked with him once on the phone, once in person, Todd was asking for advice."

Charles had moved to the edge of his seat like I had all this helpful information and he couldn't wait for me to continue.

"Advice about what?"

"Don't know."

"What kind of investigator are you?"

"I'm not one," I said, reminding him for roughly the billionth time. "Mike couldn't say because of attorney client privilege."

"That's all?"

"Well no, he told Todd never to return to his house."

"Seems odd, unless Todd said something to upset Mike. And if he did, could've it been a reason for Mike to kill him?"

I said, "It's as good as any."

"What'd you think of Mike? He a good or bad witch?"

"Not sure which witch, but he seems like a man who won't take crap from anyone. He's protective of his family."

"The plot thickens. Moving on, what about the house owners?" Charles eyes narrowed.

"Not sure. They don't seem personable, but." I shrugged.

"You talked to them, talked to others about them, so you must have thoughts on Dr. Ass and his wife?"

"He seems like a condescending jerk; so, I agree with the others. When I talked to Erika, she seemed calm, like she was trying to fix everything."

"What Bri said about her, makes one wonder."

"Yes, it does, Charles, and raises more questions."

Charles stuffed a handful of chips in his mouth and mumbled, "So, who killed him?"

"Heck if I know. You're the detective, who do you think?"

"Heck if I know."

Finally, we agreed.

Chapter Twenty-One

The cold rain that covered the area yesterday was still around giving me an excuse not to venture out. After too much coffee, a bowl of Rice Krispies, and rehashing Charles and my discussion yesterday, I realized I knew little more about who might've killed Todd Lee than I did when we stumbled on the body. So, why was I thinking about it? Neither Charles nor I knew Todd Lee. We didn't know anyone who would've even considered him a friend. True, seeing him on the pantry floor left an indelible impression. Was that reason enough to be racking my brain for a way to learn the identity of his killer? On a rational level, the answer was clearly no. So, why was I sitting here on a rainy morning thinking about it? On the other hand, what harm would it do if I asked questions of the people who knew Mr. Lee?

Who did I know who might have known one or more of the potential suspects who might've had reason to kill Lee?

The police believed Jeff Hildebrand was the killer. He spent several nights sleeping in the haunted house as did the victim. He admitted removing evidence from the house that would've proven he'd been there. I didn't know Hildebrand nor anyone who knew him well. He was by far the lead suspect.

The only people I knew who knew Fred Robinson and his wife beyond a casual knowledge were John and Bri Rice. After the good Dr. Robinson shut down the haunted house, John and Bri were angry with them. Did they know more than they'd shared? Regardless what John and Bri knew about the Robinson's, what motive would either of the Robinson's have for wanting Lee dead? After all, his death hurt Fred Robinson's reputation, or so he thought, bothering him enough to shut down the popular attraction.

Thinking of John and Bri, did they have reason to want Lee dead? Even if one or both had reason, killing him in the house where they were working wouldn't have been wise. He'd worked for them a week on top of his previous exchanges with Bri in Charleston. There was bad blood between the Rices and Lee. It was a long shot, but my friend and former Realtor Bob Howard might know the couple since they had a renovations' business. A quick call could answer that question. Any answer was better than the ones I had no answer for.

"Bob," I said when he answered the phone with the country sounds of Mel Tillis playing in the background. "How's the world of a bar owner?"

Bob retired from a successful career as a Realtor to buy Al's Bar, a rundown restaurant and bar owned by Al Washington, Bob's unlikely friend. Bob knew as much about running a bar as an elephant does about entering a spelling bee but bought the business because his friend was in poor health.

"Couldn't be better. Hell, there were seven people in yesterday for lunch. Damned gold mine."

I coughed back a laugh. "Great."

George Jones replaced Mel Tillis singing in the background, and Bob said, "You ain't with the freakin' IRS, so why are you pestering me about business?"

"Do you know John and Bri Rice, they own J&B Renovations?"

"Yes."

"What do you know about them?"

"Chris, you sound like you need a cheeseburger."

"Sounds like a good idea."

"Good, if you hurry, I can hold off the crowd enough to save you a seat."

I took the subtle hint—subtle for Bob—and said, "See you in a little while."

Al's Bar is in a concrete block building it shares with a Laundromat a block off Calhoun Street near downtown Charleston. Both businesses have been in continuous operation longer than most college students have been alive.

Al met me at the door. He was in his early eighties with short, gray hair, coffee stained teeth, and skin between dark brown and light black. He pushed out of the ancient chair stationed by the door so he could greet guests without taxing his arthritic knees. After Bob bought the business, Al agreed to stay on and function as greeter so he would have somewhere to go, and to serve as peacekeeper between the mostly African American customer base and Bob, whose skin color would make a marshmallow appear gray.

"Thank goodness, you're here," Al said as he gave me a

hug. "Your buddy's been moaning and groaning, wondering if you'd ever show. He's been pestering the lunch crowd about it for the last forever." Al pointed to the "lunch crowd," consisting of four men seated at a table beside the window. Bob was at his table near the back of the room. I knew it was *his table* because he'd installed a plaque announcing its vaulted status.

"Get back here and stop gabbing with the hired help!" Bob bellowed, drawing the attention of the *lunch crowd*.

Bob was in his late seventies, six-foot-tall, burly, saying it kindly, wearing a Hawaiian flowery shirt, and most likely shorts, although I couldn't see his legs stuffed between the table and his chair.

"About time you got here," he said in his best customer unfriendly voice. "Hey, you behind the grill, fix my friend a cheeseburger, two helpings of fries, and a glass of cheap wine."

Lawrence, Al's part time cook and person Bob knows the name of as well as he knew mine, said, "Yes, Master Bob."

"Great guy," Bob said as his attention drifted to me. "Don't know what I'd do without him."

"I'm sure he knows how much you appreciate him," I said, oozing sarcasm.

"Smart ass."

I smiled.

"You and your quarter wit friends trying to catch who killed the stiff that wasn't supposed to be part of that haunted house over your way?"

"Why ask that?"

"Let's see. First, I read in the paper about a body found in a haunted house on your little island. Then, you call asking if I know the guys who own J&B Renovations, the company that happens to be fixing up the house where the stiff was found. Finally, you and your eighth wit friend have a way of snooping into things you shouldn't be snooping into. How am I doing so far?"

Lawrence arrived with my cheeseburger, wine, and more fries than I could eat at one meal, although I knew Bob didn't order the double helping for me. I thanked Lawrence and being the wise man I knew him to be, he headed back to the kitchen before Bob could shower him with more love.

"Well," Bob said as I took a bite of burger, "how was I doing?"

"I met John and Bri at the house the other day and was curious if you knew them. I figured since they did renovations, you might've met them during your successful career in real estate. Nothing more."

Bob grabbed one of my fries, stuck it in his mouth, and said, "What a crock. You forget you're talking to old Bob, the guy who saved your bacon more than once when you stuck your nose where it didn't belong?"

"What do you know about them?" I said, skipping over the crock comment.

He smiled like I'd agreed with his assessment about why I was asking about the Rices. "The last two McMansions I brokered the sale of before I became a restaurant magnet needed extensive work. I'd heard good things about J&B, so I recommended them to the homeowners. Because I was such a brilliant and successful Realtor, the homeowners asked me to meet with John and Bri to make sure they were legitimate." He grabbed another fry and yelled for Lawrence to bring him another beer.

"What did you learn about John and Bri?"

"From them, little. They told me they were well respected, had a brag book filled with photos of successful, beautiful, functional, blah, blah, blah renovations they'd done. I didn't see any photos of them killing anyone in one of their renovated houses."

"Disappointing."

"Smart ass."

Over the years, I'd convinced myself that was one of Bob's terms of endearment, so I ignored it. "You said, you learned little from them, implying you learned more from others?"

"I can't sneak anything past you."

I grinned as Charlie Rich sang "Behind Closed Doors" from the jukebox.

The song selection was one of several sticking points between Bob and his customers. As a concession to their friendship, years ago, Al salted the jukebox with many of Bob's favorite country songs, or according to Bob, the only kind of songs. They may be the only kind of songs to Bob's ears, but to most of Al's customers, they wouldn't reach the top million in songs they'd play.

"The references John and Bri shared gave glowing comments about the company, their work, on and on."

"Bob, before we die of old age, could you get to the point?"

He sighed. "Being as brilliant as I am, I'd never limit my reference checking to the names given to me by the person I was checking on."

"Brilliant idea."

"Smart ass. Anyway, I called a couple of professional acquaintances to see if they knew of J&B. They didn't have anything bad to say about the company's work, but they both said John was weird. Only one of them knew Bri, but he used a similar description plus a few other things about her."

"Weird?"

"Seems that renovations aren't their only business. Lowcountry Paranormal Investigations is what they really love doing. Seems the renovators are obsessed with the paranormal. Ghosts, things that go bump in the night, dead people returning to haunt us normal folks."

"Bob, a lot of people are into the paranormal. How does that make the Rices weird?"

He stuffed two more fries into his mouth, washed them down with beer, then leaned my direction. "Now I'm not one to judge others," He laughed. "Hell, yes I am. Whatever, apparently the Rices claim to find ghosts where no one else has. One of my acquaintances told me he heard they killed a goat and stuck it in someone's attic, so they could find it and say the former homeowner was a goatherder and his ghost must've killed the animal."

"You believe your friend?"

"Acquaintance, not friend, but hell, who knows. John Rice claims he's a paranormalist, but if you ask me, he's a paraabnormalist."

"Bob, do you think John or Bri could've killed the man in the haunted house because they caught him squatting in there when they were hunting ghosts?"

Bob took another drag off his beer, looked toward Al at the door, turned to me, and said, "I think that'd be one stupid reason to kill someone, but anything's possible. What do you think?"

"Seems unlikely, but possible."

"There you go. Your good buddy Bob solves another murder you're sticking your nose into."

"Don't know how I could do it without you."

"Smart ass."

I agreed.

"One more thing," Bob said, "Not that this is proof of anything, but if you ask me, anyone who'd kill a helpless goat then sticks it in someone's attic, has a screw or two loose. Anyone with a screw or two loose can kill a person. You can put money on it."

"You said one of your friends, umm, acquaintances said more about Bri. What about her?"

Bob smiled. "Said she was one hot, blond, renovating chick."

I finished my cheeseburger, Bob finished the mound of fries, and Tammy Wynette finished "Stand By Your Man." Bob added if I wasn't going to spend any more money, I'd better get back to catching a killer. He said I was taking up a chair that could be holding someone's rear end; someone who could be putting money in Bob's pocket. I didn't point out that there were roughly thirty empty chairs in the room.

Before I left, Bob said, "Try not to get yourself killed trying to catch the killer."

Bob could always be counted on for helpful advice.

On the drive home, I wasn't trying to catch a killer, but trying to figure out if he'd said anything helpful, when the phone interrupted my thoughts.

Chief LaMond responded to my "Hello," with, "Catch you at a bad time?"

"No, was on my way home from Al's."

"Crap, I wanted to catch you at a bad time. You a cheeseburger heavier?"

"Yes, anything else you wanted to know?"

"That's more than I wanted to know, but I called to tell you Jeff Hildebrand was released on bail this morning."

"There's nothing to hold him on the murder?"

"Other than Detective Adair being convinced he did it, no. Again, that pesky concept of proof evades the Sheriff's Office. Hildebrand's evidence tampering trial won't be held for a couple of months. Since he already told Adair he did it, even our imperfect court system will have a hard time getting that wrong."

"Where's Hildebrand now?"

"Who knows. He was told not to leave the country, which was a joke. A homeless man with no wallet, probably doesn't have a passport or the bucks to fly off to Tanzania."

"Cindy, thanks for letting me know."

"You know I live for telling you stuff that's none of your business."

She hung up before I could echo Bob and call her a smart ass.

I was pulling in the drive when the phone rang again.

"Is this Chris Landrum?"

I said it was.

"Chris, this is Mike Stone. Did I catch you at a bad time?"

Wow, two civil conversation beginnings during one car ride. I assured him it wasn't.

"Good. Is there a chance you could meet me tomorrow? Something I'd like to talk to you about."

"Sure."

"Can you stop by the house around two?"

"Yes, is there anything I need to know before then?" I asked, rather than blurting out, *Why would you want to meet with me?*

"Umm, no. We can talk about it tomorrow."

Chapter Twenty-Two

Puzzling dreams and unsettling periods between sleep and being awake filled the night. I couldn't put my finger on anything specific, but it was far from normal. My guess was the uneasiness was caused by the pending meeting with Mike Stone. But why? The Stone family was pleasant. Desmond was strange, but from my brief encounters with him I couldn't tell if he was simply being a rebellious teen or something more sinister. Today at two, I agreed to enter the lair of the witch, correction four witches, and, oh yeah, a dog bigger than a Fiat. Aren't witches supposed to have cats, cats that can't put your whole head in their mouth? Enough! If I keep on this path, I'll cancel the meeting. I'm being ridiculous.

Heading to Bert's for coffee and human interaction will force me back to reality.

As soon as I entered the store, I was greeted with, "Morning, Chris."

"Roger."

He looked out the door then at me. "I'm standing here waiting for the storm."

I didn't remember asking him what he was doing. "Storm?"

"Chris, head to the Pier and look at those storm clouds rolling in." Roger nodded towards the door.

"Sounds like a plan, but first, coffee."

I drew a cup then walked toward the Pier. Off in the distance, I saw what Roger was talking about. Thick black clouds filled the space the early morning sun normally occupied. Instead of venturing on the Pier, I leaned against the railing overlooking the massive structure. Three fishermen headed my way, probably with little to show for their efforts. The wind had kicked up and the distant skies were so dark it made me think of Halloween. I stood watching the thunderheads rolling my way and was mesmerized by the life the clouds took on. When lightening appeared closer than I was comfortable with, I headed home.

By the time I reached my cottage, the rain arrived, deafening thunder vibrated in my ears. It was fortunate I hadn't walked to the far end of the Pier. October had finally shown its natural colors with a vengeance. I couldn't have picked a better setting to meet a witch than a stormy afternoon in late October.

My lack of sleep must've caught up with me since the next thing I remembered was waking up in my chair in the living room with ten minutes to get to Mike's house. I headed to the car and was surprised the rain had stopped; however, thunder was still protesting and the petrichor of rain still filled the air. Roger should get a second job as a meteorologist since he predicted the storm when today's weather gurus had called for partly cloudy with a zero percent chance of precipitation.

On the short drive, I continued wondering what Mike wanted to share. Surely, he wasn't going to breach attorney client privilege and tell me about his conversations with Todd Lee. Or was he?

I pulled in the Stone's drive and parked behind Banshee. I sat in my car a minute admiring Mike's classic ride, then realized I couldn't stall any longer. On the way to the front door, it entered my mind that I should've brought a bone for Lugh. I smiled wondering where I could get a Titanosaurus bone, one that's big enough for the Irish Wolfhound.

I'd passed the front of the classic Mustang when something caught my eye. I slowly turned to face the car where I saw Mike sitting in the driver's seat.

"Mike, I didn't see you there."

He didn't answer. I returned to the open driver's side window, bent down to say something, when the words stuck in my throat. Mike leaned to the left; a thin stream of blood ran down the side of his face.

I stepped back, tripped over one of the large rocks lining the edge of the drive, and landed on my shoulder in Shannon's flower garden. Not bothering to stand, I grabbed my phone and called Cindy.

She answered with, "Didn't I just talk to you yesterday?" She laughed then added, "What do you want now?"

"Cindy, Mike Stone's dead. You need to get here."

"You sure?"

"Dead certain."

"Where?"

"His house, in the driveway. He's in his car."

"I know where it is. We're on our way. Are you alone?"

"Think so."

"Don't touch anything. Sit in your car and wait for the cavalry. You hear me, don't do anything."

Cindy didn't have to tell me twice. I pushed myself up off the wet ground, looked at Mike one more time, and on wobbly legs, returned to my car. I got in and locked the door. I fought the urge to slam it in reverse, head home, while trying to block out the sight of seeing Mike in his classic car, one he'd never drive again.

I was jolted out of my grim thoughts by sirens heading my way. Cindy wasn't joking about the cavalry. It seemed like the entire police force and fire vehicles were lining the street in front of the house. Cindy approached my door, pulled the handle, but finding it locked, tapped on the window.

"Hop out and come with me."

I stepped out slowly, making sure my legs would hold me. Cindy grabbed my arm and led me to her pickup truck.

She said, "Stay here."

The Chief and two of her officers looked in Mike's vehicle. Cindy shook her head then told one of the officers to stay with the body while she and Officer Spencer headed to the house with firearms drawn. When they reached the door, Officer Spencer turned the knob while the Chief stood on the opposite side of the entry. It opened and Lugh loped past them and bolted for the Mustang. The huge dog stuck his head in the window nudging Mike, then sat and let out a mournful howl. I was watching Lugh and missed seeing Cindy and Spencer enter the house.

Moments later, Spencer came out with Desmond. Cindy followed. Desmond showed no emotion as he looked towards the Mustang. Spencer lightly gripped the boy's elbow and turned him away from the car before escorting the emotionless young man to a police cruiser parked at the street.

Cindy joined me. "Up to answering questions?"

I nodded.

"Let's start with, what in holy hell's going on?"

"Mike called yesterday asking me to meet him. We agreed to meet here at two o'clock. I showed up. You know the rest."

"And lo and behold, you find another body, your favorite pastime."

I closed my eyes and shook my head. My stomach churned.

"Sorry, bad joke," she said and patted my arm. "Did you know Desmond was here? Do you know where the rest of the family is?"

"No to both questions."

Lugh's bark, roughly the same volume as the earlier thunder, drew our attention to the driveway. Two paramedics were trying to get to Mike. Lugh was standing guard, teeth bared, not letting anyone near the car.

One of the paramedics yelled. "Chief, what do you want us to do?"

"Chris, do you know the dog well enough to get him?"

"No, ma'am. I'm in no hurry to meet my maker. His name is Lugh if that helps."

"It doesn't." Cindy looked around as if she were searching for the perfect dog wrangler.

Before someone was chosen to be sacrificed, I heard a familiar voice and phrase from behind Cindy's vehicle.

"*Eist liom!*"

Lugh turned toward the voice then ran to Shannon's

side as she stared at the Mustang. Roisin peeked around from behind her mother.

My heart sank. Their world was about to be forever changed.

Cindy approached the new arrivals to block their view of the car. "Mrs. Stone, I'm Chief LaMond. I need to speak to you over here." Cindy tried to turn Shannon away from the yard and driveway.

Shannon wasn't having it. "Chief LaMond," she said in a strong, seemingly emotionless voice, "please allow me to go see my husband."

"I don't think that's a good idea. Let them take care of Mr. Stone."

Thinking a friendly face may be some solace, I walked over to help Cindy move the ladies from the awful scene.

Offering the best smile I could manage under the circumstances, I said, "Shannon, Roisin, I think it'd be best if you go with the Chief."

Shannon glared at me, stared at the sky, then said, "You're right, Chris. Chief, where would you like us to go?"

"Mrs. Stone, it would be best if we go to my office. You and your daughter can ride with me."

"Please call me Shannon," she said as she stroked Lugh's head. I would rather drive; besides, I don't want to leave Lugh here."

"I don't think you should be driving. I can have an officer drive your car." Cindy looked around to see who was available.

Shannon looked at me. "Chris, would you drive us to Chief LaMond's office?"

Before I answered, Cindy said it was a good idea and suggested we head out and let everyone do what needed to be done at the house. Officer Spencer had already left with Desmond.

I followed mother and daughter to their red Ford EcoSport. Roisin opened the tailgate and Lugh stepped in and laid down. I got in and waited for Shannon, who stood looking at the driveway until Roisin touched her arm and they both entered the SUV. The ride to Cindy's office was silent except the haunting notes of a pan flute coming from the speakers.

I parked near the entry to the Department of Public Safety, handed Shannon the keys, and said, "Shannon, I'll head home now. If you need anything, please call." I started to give her my number.

"Please go with us, Mr. Chris. Please," Roisin said as she looked at me in the rearview mirror.

Shannon said, "I hate to ask, Chris, but I'd feel more comfortable if you came with us."

"Of course."

We looked like a mismatched foursome heading into Cindy's office with Lugh leading the way, followed by Shannon, Roisin, then me. Cindy smiled at me as she closed the door behind us.

The Chief's office was large but with all of us packed in it felt cramped, especially with Lugh taking up the space of three large adults.

"We asked Chris to be here, Chief LaMond," Shannon said. "Hope you don't mind."

"Shannon, that's fine."

"Chief LaMond, please tell me what happened to my husband?"

"We're not sure. I'm so sorry. Shannon, I know this is a

terrible time, but I need to get some information. Could you answer some questions?"

Shannon nodded.

In a soft voice, Cindy said, "When did you leave the house today?"

Shannon lowered her head and put her hands over her face. Roisin sat with one hand on Lugh's head, her other hand wiping away tears. I didn't think Shannon was going to answer until she jerked her head up and said, "We left for Charleston around ten-thirty; went shopping for herbs and Roisin wanted to find some crystals."

Cindy said, "I know this is hard, Shannon. What about your son? Did he go with you?"

Shannon said, "Desmond doesn't go shopping with us if he can get out of it."

Roisin chimed in before her mom continued, "He was going to the lighthouse with some guys."

Shannon reached for her phone. "I need to call him, so he doesn't go home."

Cindy held up her hand. "Shannon, your son is with one of my officers. He was in his room when we arrived at your house." Cindy waited for Shannon's response.

"He knows?" Shannon said, then stared out the window.

Cindy said, "Yes."

"Shannon," I said, "did you know I was going to meet Mike today?"

Cindy gave me a sideways glance I translated as *I'm doing the questioning.*

"Yes, he told me last night, but didn't say why. I assumed it was about Todd, umm, the dead man from the haunted house."

Cindy's look my direction now became a *what have you*

done now? She then turned to Shannon. "Was your husband home when you left for Charleston?"

"Yes, he was going to run to Harris Teeter and the post office but wouldn't have been gone long."

Cindy said, "Do you know anyone who might have wanted to harm Mike?"

A tear rolled down her cheek, and in a voice barely above a whisper, said, "No, he was a gentle soul, never crossed anyone."

"Not even at work?" Cindy said, and jotted something on her legal pad.

Cindy's phone rang before Shannon answered. "Yeah," she said into the mouthpiece. I could hear the faint voice of the other person on the line but couldn't make out what he was saying. Cindy said, "Fifteen minutes, conference room," then returned the phone to the desk before turning to Shannon. "Sorry, you were saying?"

"Law was Mike's profession. He did it well, but he made no enemies. Again, he's a gentle soul." Shannon's hand went to Lugh's head. The protective canine had risen when her voice grew louder.

Roisin placed her hand on her mother's hand then locked on the Chief. "Chief LaMond, do you have more questions, or can we go?"

Cindy appeared stunned by the question posed by the youngest person in the room but smiled at Roisin. "Detective Adair from the Sheriff's Office will be here in a few minutes and needs to talk with both of you. Let me take you to a room where you'll be able to talk."

Shannon slowly stood.

"Shannon," I said, "do you want me to drive you somewhere after you're done here?"

"Chris, you have done more than enough. We'll be fine, thank you."

Shannon, Roisin, and Lugh left with Cindy. I remained in the office and waited for the Chief to return.

Ten minutes later, she returned, flopped down in her chair, then said, "Ok, what do you make of all that?"

I didn't answer fast enough.

"Chris."

"Sorry, didn't know where to start. Didn't even know if you wanted my input."

"I never want your input but has that ever stopped you?"

I smiled. "I found it strange she didn't ask anything more about Desmond, things like where he was, why he wasn't in the room with the rest of us?"

Cindy said, "That was strange, but I don't know how someone should act after learning her husband, the father of her two kids, was dead." She stood and added, "Let's go, I'll take you to your car."

"Thanks, but I'll walk."

Cindy smiled. "Don't think for a second I'm going to let you go back to a crime scene without adult supervision."

I thought it best not to mention that I was almost old enough to be her father. I quickly fell in step beside the Chief on the way to her truck. The ride to the Stone house was almost as quiet as the ride from the house to Cindy's office, only static from the police radio broke the silence. Cindy pulled up behind my car where I saw crime scene tape around Mike's car and the house. A crime scene tech from Charleston was carrying two large aluminum cases from the van toward the Mustang.

Cindy said, "Get out, go home, rest. That's an order from your wise Police Chief."

I saluted. "Yes, sir."

"Smart ass."

As I left the latest homicide scene on Folly Beach, I found myself with more questions and more sadness.

Then the sky unleashed a torrential downpour.

What could happen next?

Chapter Twenty-Three

My legs were still not hike worthy when I arrived home. I grabbed a bottle of tea from the nearly empty refrigerator and moved to the living room. Unfortunately, Mike Stone wasn't the first dead body I'd run across since I'd moved to Folly. In fact, it wasn't the first in the last couple of weeks, but it was the first of someone who'd asked me to meet with him a few hours before his last breath. And, seeing the traumatized, grieving look on Shannon and Roisin's faces, his death struck me harder than the others.

Thinking of Roisin's pain, I knew there was someone I had to call to let him know what had happened, that is, if he didn't already know.

The phone rang five times without an answer, so I was afraid I was going to get voicemail, until a breathless Preacher Burl said, "Hey, Brother Chris, give me a second to catch my breath." The second turned into a minute before Burl said, "Sorry, I just returned from Harris Teeter and was carrying in groceries. To this old preacher, these steps get higher each time I climb them."

"Want me to call back?"

"No, no, let me throw this milk in the refrigerator and I'm all ears." He laughed. "Well, all ears and an out of shape body."

"I know the feeling, Preacher."

He laughed again then said, "What did I do to have the honor of your call?"

I knew my next words would erase all humor from my friend.

"Preacher, Mike Stone was killed today."

"Oh, my Lord, please tell me you're not serious."

"Afraid so. I found him in his car at their house."

"What happened? Was Roisin there? Umm, and, of course, Shannon and Desmond?"

I told him where the family members had been and about what I assumed to be a fatal gunshot wound to the head.

"Brother Chris, anyone know what occurred? Who did it? Why?"

"Preacher, at this point, I don't think there are answers. The family is meeting with the detective from the Sheriff's Office at City Hall. I assume they'll go home after that." I hesitated before saying, "I don't know what kind of spiritual guidance you could offer, but Roisin feels close to you, so you may want to call or visit."

"Brother Chris, regardless of beliefs, we all grieve. Sister Roisin is a sensitive young lady who is quite vulnerable. This will touch her deeply. I'd like to be there when they return, so I best head that way now. Roisin and the family need a friend even if we don't have the same spiritual guidepost."

"Preacher, I know she'll appreciate it. Please let me know if there's anything I can do to help."

He said he would.

I didn't know if it was still storming but knew that unless I informed Charles immediately, I'd incur a torrential downpour of Charles. I was also hungry.

My friend was quicker to answer than Burl had been. In the spirit of if you can't beat them, join them, I took a page out of Charles's phone conversation playbook and began with, "Mike Stone's dead. Meet me at Cal's."

"What? How?"

I hung up with those questions unanswered, for now.

———

It was early for Cal's bar crowd. Three tables were occupied, and two men were in deep discussion as they leaned against the bar. From the jukebox, Don Gibson was sharing his version of "Sweet Dreams;" Cal was sliding a bottle of beer to one of the men at the bar; and Charles was standing by the door wearing a cherry red, long sleeve sweatshirt with the University of New Mexico in small letters under what appeared to be an angry dog like animal.

Charles's mouth imitated the creatures snarl when he glanced at his wrist before saying, "What took you so long?"

I didn't think fifteen minutes from the time I hung up was that long, but I'd be wasting my time sharing that observation.

"Glad you could make it, Charles."

He turned to Cal. "Bring my tardy friend a glass of your finest red wine. We'll be at that table by the wall unless Chris gets lost on the way."

I arrived at the designated table the same time Charles made the long twenty-five-foot walk, thirty seconds before Cal set my wine in front of me and handed a beer to Charles.

Charles pointed to the creature on his sweatshirt. "It's a lobo, that's Spanish for wolf, in case you were going to ask."

I wasn't and stared at him.

"Spill it," he said after giving me a second to absorb the Spanish lesson. "Mike Stone. How do you know he's dead? What happened? Who killed him? How's Lugh?" Charles took a breath long enough for me to hear Connie Smith singing "Once a Day," before adding, "Did I already say spill it?"

That was my cue to begin—begin until he interrupted countless times. I started by telling him how Mike had called to ask me to meet him. Charles's first interruption came when he demanded to know why I hadn't invited him to the meeting. Because Mike had asked me was my obvious response, but knew it wouldn't fly, so I skipped saying it and proceeded to tell him what had happened and what little I'd learned from being there finding the body.

After going over the story and assuring him Lugh was fine, he said, "Think it had something to do with what he was going to tell you?"

"That's possible."

"Who knew you were meeting him?"

"Shannon."

"What about the kids?"

"Don't know, probably."

"And Desmond wasn't in Charleston with his mother and sister?"

"No, as I said, he was at the house when I found the body."

"In the house where you saw an ice pick, an ice pick like one that stabbed Todd Lee."

"An ice pick you pointed out like one that could be found in most any house here."

"He was at the house, the others were shopping in Charleston, while his dad was killed in the driveway, feet away from where he was. Super sized coincidence if you ask me."

"What motive would Mike's sixteen-year-old have for killing his father?"

"Don't know, but it wouldn't be the first time a teenager bumped off his pop."

"Okay, I'll concede it's possible."

"How're we going to prove it?"

"We've been over this. I don't know."

Cal returned to the table and asked if we needed anything else. My stomach reminded me that food was the reason I wanted to come to Cal's in the first place. I told him a cheeseburger and fries. Charles asked if I was buying. I nodded and he said he'd have the same. Charles watched the owner head to the kitchen, tapped me on the arm, and said, "Isn't that Nate Davis heading to the bar?"

I twisted around to see who he was talking about. "Yes."

That's all it took for Charles to jump up, rush to the bar, and return with Nate by his side.

"Chris, guess what? Nate said he could join us. I ordered him a burger and told Cal to put it on your tab."

Lacking an ice pick to stick in my friend, I smiled and welcomed Nate.

"Nate," Charles said, "you know Mike Stone?"

"Don't think so. Who's he?"

"An attorney who lived over here. He was killed today."

A cheerful way to start a conversation, I thought.

"Oh," Nate said. "Who did it?"

"Don't know," Charles said and nodded toward me. "Chris found the body."

Nate turned to me. "That's terrible. Are you okay?"

I told him I was then noted that was a question Charles hadn't asked.

After I shared with Nate what I knew of the tragic event, Cal arrived with our food and asked if we needed anything else. None of us did, so he returned to the bar. We each took a bite, before Charles said, "Nate, seems the last time we were in here, you were talking about Todd Lee."

Nate took a sip of beer then pointed the top of the bottle at Charles. "Yes. You think the guy murdered today had something to do with Lee's killing?"

"It could," Charles said. "Mind telling us again what you knew about Lee?"

He took another bite before saying, "Think I told you all of it. He was a jerk."

"Didn't you say something about a secret that'd make him rich?"

"He said it several times, and I didn't have much to do with him."

"What do you think he meant?"

"Don't know for sure, mind you, but think it had something to do with him blackmailing someone."

I didn't recall everything he'd told us before but was certain blackmail wasn't mentioned.

I said, "What made you think that?"

"Look, Chris, I don't know about you fellas, but I don't

remember everything someone says to me." He nodded toward the bar. "Hell, I don't remember everything Cal and I said to each other when I came in today. The jerk only worked for J&B a week. He said a lot of stuff like guys working together do. Helps kill time, you know."

Charles said, "So you don't remember what he said about blackmail?"

Nate took two more bites as he stared at Charles like *that's what I just said.*

"How's the remodel coming?" I said to move the conversation forward without belaboring what he'd said he didn't remember.

"Fine, I guess. Lately, the Robinson's are hovering over us like that'll get the job done faster. Don't know how John and Bri put up with it. Glad it ain't my company." He glanced at his watch. "Guys, gotta run. Thanks for the food and drink. Maybe I'll run into you again."

After he left, Charles said, "He sure got in a hurry to get out of here. Think he killed the two men?"

"No reason to think so. He probably wasn't a fan of being interrogated."

"Got him a free meal. What more could he want?" He didn't wait for my response. "Think he's right about Todd Lee blackmailing someone? It'd be a good reason to kill him."

"Yes, but who?"

That question remained unanswered as I left Cal's to Johnny Cash singing "Guess Things Happen That Way."

Chapter Twenty-Four

After finding Mike's body, going to Chief LaMond's office with the grieving Shannon and Roisin, calling Burl to tell him the horrible news, and, of course, Charles's interrogation, I was looking forward to a peaceful morning at home. If the weather held, I could take my neglected camera for a stroll to get back to some semblance of normalcy.

Of course, as the saying goes, life happens while we're busy making other plans. On the way to the spare bedroom to retrieve my camera, I heard a faint knock at the front door, so faint I doubted my ears, then I heard it again. Grabbing my camera, I went to the door wondering who would be gently knocking since most of my friends who stopped by seemed more irritated to find the door locked and pounded on it.

I opened the door to, "Good morning, Mr. Chris," Roisin said as softly as her knock.

"Roisin, nice to see you," I said, trying to hide my

surprise that the young lady was standing on my front porch after yesterday's tragic event.

"I don't want to bother you but knew this was the place I needed to be. Is it okay?"

Before I answered, her gaze went to my camera and I saw a twinkle in her eyes.

"I'm heading out to take some photos along the beach. Would you like to join me?"

Roisin smiled. "I'd love to."

I grabbed my windbreaker and met her in the yard.

"Do you take many pictures?" she asked, her voice stronger than at first.

"Not as many as I used to. It's a passion of mine and one I enjoy when I can get out."

Roisin smiled. "I love going into nature and taking memory photos."

"Memory photos?"

"Mr. Chris, we don't have an excess of material things." She hesitated and tapped the side of her head. "My pictures are stored in my mind."

"That makes sense, until you get my age when the mind will delete the photos before you get home."

My new young friend chuckled. "You're funny." We walked a few more steps before she added, "Guess you want to know why I appeared at your door." She looked down at her sandals as she walked beside me.

"Yes. It's not often that I see such a lovely young lady standing on my porch."

Except for a quick smile, she didn't say anything for a block, so I was about to ask which way she would like to head when the silence was broken.

"I don't get along with many people. I prefer animals

and being in nature, that's where I belong. People find me strange, and that's okay."

I found it strange that she hadn't mentioned anything about her dad, but instead of mentioning it, I said, "You aren't strange, maybe just different than others your age. That's a good thing."

"Nice of you to say. Umm, that brings me to the reason I appeared on your porch without benefit of an invitation. Preacher Burl has become my best friend and he brought you into our lives. I find you to be a nice soul, someone I can talk to and not be judged."

I nodded as we followed the footpath to the beach.

"I, umm, we would like you to attend Dad's funeral service. Preacher Burl will be there and a few others, but I need you there." Roisin stopped and looked at me as if she were pleading for a positive response.

"Of course. I'd be honored, but why do you say you need me there?"

"You found Dad. You were the first good person he saw after the evilness that took him."

"Saw?"

"Sorry, I forgot you don't know our beliefs. Death isn't the ending but a new beginning."

"I didn't realize."

"We don't fear death, Mr. Chris. We are forever connected to those who have gone to the afterlife."

"When and where will the funeral be?"

She twisted her foot in the sand. "He's being cremated today. The funeral will be tomorrow morning at eleven." She looked up from the sand and smiled. "In the back garden."

We continued along the shore taking photos of the sea

and birds, me, with my camera, Roisin in her mind. She pointed out potential shots I hadn't noticed. It was a pleasant stroll with a young lady who appeared to have a better grasp on life and death than most adults I know. After an hour, my legs reminded me I wasn't as young as I used to be.

"Roisin, I need to head home, besides I'm sure your family is wondering where you are."

"Mom knows I came to see you. She doesn't worry unless it gets dark, and Desmond is not even home."

"Where's your brother?" I asked, wondering when I started sounding like Charles.

She shrugged. "Yesterday, after we left that nice Police Chief's office, Desmond wouldn't speak to Mom or me. We got home and he went to his room, slammed the door, didn't come out all night. Mom went to check on him this morning. He was gone."

"Is that normal for him to disappear?"

"Mom told me he needed time to cope with someone, umm, killing our father. She said he'd be back." Roisin shook her head.

"Don't you believe her?"

"Oh, I guess, but he's been acting strange, okay stranger than usual since we went to the haunted house. Now this."

"Sorry."

I placed my hand on her shoulder. She took a deep breath and exhaled. It was easy to forget she was an eleven-year-old with her entire world in turmoil, with dark days ahead.

We walked back towards the Pier. When we got under the wooden structure, she looked around as if she just realized where we were.

"Mr. Chris, we will part ways here. I must head home. You can finish your planned day."

"I can walk you home if you like. It's no trouble."

"That's kind of you, but I'm fine." She stopped, stared at me, and said, "Mr. Chris, do you know who killed Dad?"

I was so close to escaping without this sweet young lady asking me the question I'd asked myself countless times since yesterday afternoon.

"Roisin, I'm afraid I have no idea."

"I was hoping you knew."

"Why would you think I might know?"

"Not sure. Dad has been in a different place, sort of not his happy self when he talked to Mom. After meeting you it seemed to bring some grounding to his soul."

"Did he explain his mood change?"

"No. It seemed to start after I heard him talking to someone on the phone. He had this, umm, funny sound in his voice. A sound I hadn't heard before. I had a feeling something was not right. I thought you might know something since Dad was going to talk to you yesterday."

"Who was he talking to on the phone?"

Instead of answering, a tear rolled down her cheek. She said, "I need to get home, see you tomorrow. Thank you for the adventure."

She pivoted and walked away.

It seems every conversation I have leaves me with more questions than answers. Looking at my watch and listening to my stomach growl gave me one answer. It was time for lunch. I was already out, so I might as well treat myself instead of slaving over a hot stove, okay, cold slice of bologna.

Amber's smiling face greeted me at the Dog.

She looked past me, shook her head, and said, "Table for one?"

"Yes, thank goodness."

"Have a spat with your bestie?"

She didn't wait for an answer. She took my elbow, ushered me to a table and asked if I wanted the usual. I nodded and she left to put in my order. It's nice when some things are always the same, bringing balance to life, even if that balance is going to lunch.

I pondered the morning while scrolling through the morning's photos on my camera. One was of Roisin staring at the ocean with a look of wisdom and sorrow on her face. Strange, I don't recall snapping it.

"Nice shot, who's the girl?"

I almost dropped the camera. I hadn't heard Amber arrive with my iced tea. Jumpiness seems to be my middle name this month. I'll be glad when Halloween is over and I can concentrate on something positive like, well, like anything but Halloween.

"That's Roisin Stone."

"Any relation to the man killed yesterday on East Huron?" she asked as she continued looking at the camera's monitor.

"His daughter. She came to the house this morning to invite me to the funeral."

"So, besides finding the body you're asked to the funeral. I didn't know you knew the witchy family."

"Amber, is there anything you don't know on this island, beside me knowing the Stones?"

"Don't know who killed Mr. Stone or the guy in the haunted house. That's up to you and Charles to figure out."

"The man in the haunted house is Todd Lee, and it's the job for the police to figure out who killed both men."

She grinned. "Keep telling yourself that."

The remainder of my lunch was filled with my sandwich and numerous thoughts. Who was Mike talking to on the phone? Was it Todd, and if so, who were they talking about? How did Roisin hear the conversation? Who might be next to die, and why? What is a Wiccan funeral like? I finished lunch with no significant questions answered, so I decided the best thing to do was go home.

My phone rang as I opened the door.

"Brother Chris, did I catch you at a bad time?"

"No Preacher, what can I do for you?"

"Wanted to let you know tomorrow is Brother Mike's funeral."

"I know, Roisin stopped by today to invite me."

"Oh," He sounded surprised. "That's good. I was at their house most of the morning helping Shannon. I'll see you tomorrow?"

"Was Desmond there?"

"No. Shannon was vague about his location, and I didn't want to appear pushy."

"That's quite unpreacher-like."

"True, Brother Chris, but I had the feeling we should let sleeping dogs lie. Oh, speaking of dogs, Shannon asked me to invite Brother Charles to the funeral."

"Charles will love being compared to a dog."

"Funny, but not what I meant. Shannon thought it would be good for Lugh if Charles were there. Don't ask me why, just doing what was requested."

"See you tomorrow, Preacher. Have fun talking to Charles."

I sat in the chair in the living room waiting for the inevitable call from Charles.

The wait was short.

"Charles, how are you this afternoon?" Instead of waiting for a reply, I added, "Yes, I'll pick you up tomorrow for the funeral; no, I have no idea who killed him."

"Okay."

The phone went dead.

I smiled as I realized it was one of the fastest, most decisive calls ever with Charles. Perhaps, I'm finally getting Folly phone etiquette. By late afternoon, I realized the events of the last week had piled enough on me that bed seemed like the best alternative. It was possibly the first time since I've been an alleged adult, I've gone to bed before the first evening star was visible.

Chapter Twenty-Five

I was surprised the sun was starting to show over the ocean. I'd slept through the night even though I'd gone to bed before dark. While well rested, my stomach reminded me a need for nourishment was unmet. A trip next door to Bert's would take care of that. I was pleased the weather looked like it would remain pleasant if not somewhat overcast for Mike's funeral.

I returned home with coffee and an oversized cheese Danish, sat on the front porch, and started sorting the questions in my head. I thought about calling Cindy to see if she had any information, then realized calling the Chief before the sun was fully up would result in me receiving an unwanted message from her sharp tongue and nothing helpful. I'll wait until after the funeral.

Thinking of Mike's funeral, I realized most funerals I'd attended were held several days after the death and wondered if the timing had to do with his religion. My pondering was interrupted by an all toofamiliar voice.

"Morning, fellow detective," Charles said as he stepped on the porch, coffee in hand. "Knew you wouldn't have a cup for me, so I brought my own."

"You're right considering I wasn't going to pick you up for hours."

"What I figured," he said as he tapped his head while looking smug, at the same time offering a small smile.

I'd say Charles's appearance was surprising, but after all these years not much he did surprised me. However, his logo free pale purple turtleneck and light grey slacks, were strikingly different from his normal wardrobe.

He saw me looking at his attire. "I know you're thinking how handsome. Witch funerals are simply a transition in life, so my clothes reflect that."

I didn't laugh at his comment about being handsome, although it was tempting.

"Didn't know you were in tune with the Wiccan ways?"

"Wasn't until yesterday. I have a book about different funeral rituals. Found it under the stack of cookbooks. Didn't know I had it."

Considering the vast book collection my friend had acquired over the years, I would've been more surprised if he didn't have it.

"Sit and tell me why you're here so early."

"What could be better than two famous detectives going over the ins and outs of a case over coffee; coffee I had to bring because you wouldn't have any for me?"

"Famous?" I said instead of rolling my eyes. "Since you brought it up, I have some information."

"And it is?"

"Yesterday, Roisin Stone—"

"Roisin! What happened?"

"Charles, if you let me finish a sentence you'll know."

Charles leaned back like a boy who'd been scolded by the teacher for answering a question before it'd been asked.

"Roisin came to invite me to the funeral. During our conversation, she asked if I knew who killed her dad. I said—"

"What did you—"

"Charles, let me finish. You might want to hear what she had to say."

He sighed. "Sorry, continue."

"That's better. I told her no. Her response was, 'I hoped you knew who it was.'"

Thankfully, Charles had finished swallowing his coffee, or he might have had to change clothes after his huge exhale.

"Why does she think you'd know?"

"She knew her dad was going to talk with me and figured I might know."

Charles stared at the ceiling like he was trying to figure something out. The only sound came from two seagulls fighting over a cigarette on the side of the street. We watched the battle ending with the larger gull flying away with the prize.

Charles softly said, "Don't suppose she knew more?"

"Nope, seemed she was avoiding saying anything else."

"That's where we start, asking her everything she knows."

"You want to interrogate an eleven-year-old at her father's funeral?"

"Not interrogate. I want us to ask the young lady in the nicest possible way questions that'll help us catch her daddy's killer."

Our conversation turned to the weather; how it seemed to get warmer each year. A line from Randy Travis' song "Forever and Ever, Amen" came to mind, "As long as old men sit and talk about the weather." It must be true.

I reminded my early bird friend we couldn't be on Charles time to the funeral. Twenty minutes later, his ant in his pants routine became too much. I caved.

The drive took longer than normal since I didn't want to be first to arrive. Pulling up to the house, an uneasy feeling was growing in the pit of my stomach. I chalked it up to what awaited me at the house two days ago. The driveway was blocked by large potted flowers, so I pulled down the street and parked behind Preacher Burl's van. At least we weren't the first here. We were greeted by a galloping Lugh. I stopped midstride to let Charles take the lead.

Charles was standing upright but the Irish Wolfhound towered over him with its legs over his shoulders. I'd never been so happy to have my friend along.

Charles said, "What a good boy. Miss your daddy?"

Lugh finished welcoming us, turned, and trotted toward the back of the drive, with us bringing up the rear. Preacher Burl stood halfway up the driveway watching the dog's greeting. He said, "Shannon was correct. Lugh needed Charles here. Brother Charles, Brother Chris, glad to see you."

I said, "Nice to see you, Preacher. Any advice on what to expect?"

I wasn't sure what he knew about a Wiccan funeral but was certain it was more than I knew. Besides, I'd rather hear it from Burl than a prolonged description from Charles.

"Shannon and the kids will explain what's going on

throughout the service. We're here to show support and celebrate life."

"Kids?" I said. "Desmond's back?"

Charles shot me a look like I'd been withholding information from him—again.

Burl gazed at the house and said, "He got here an hour ago, seemed in a darker mood than usual."

I said, "Darker? Didn't think that was possible."

Charles cleared his throat to get Burl's attention. "Preacher, do you know who's going to be here?"

"Besides us, Shannon, the kids, a couple who own a metaphysical shop in Charleston, Dude. That's all I know."

I said, "Dude?"

"Brother Chris, it seems Desmond knows Dude from the beach. The young man spends quite a bit of time staring at the ocean."

Charles said, "No family?"

"Shannon told me Mike's family will be waiting until Halloween to honor his passing and even then, won't be coming here."

We were still in the driveway when Dude walked up followed by a couple I didn't recognize. From their attire and being the only people I didn't know, I concluded it was the shop owners from Charleston. The couple wore long black cloaks with detailed black embroidery down the front, and crystal pendants.

Dude flourished a bow towards the couple, followed by, "Be my pleasure to introduce the rad Darrin and Stormy."

The man took a step forward while looking at Dude like most who don't know him well do, then extended his hand towards me, "Hello, I'm Darrin, this is my wife Stormy. You are?"

"Darrin, I'm Chris Landrum, to my right is Charles Fowler, and this is Burl Costello."

Charles chuckled. "Darrin, like in *Bewitched*."

I glared at Charles. By the end of this day he might be turned into a toad, then I'd have to carry Prince Charming everywhere.

Darrin took it in stride. From his reaction, Charles wasn't the first person to make the connection.

We were saved when Shannon called to us from the porch, "If everyone will head to the garden we will begin shortly." Her Irish brogue was more pronounced today.

The six of us walked to the garden behind the house. On an ornate wooden table sat a beautiful shoebox size mahogany container with the tree of life etched on the front. Placed in a circle around the urn were clear crystals and stones. To the left and the right of the crystals and stones were candles, along with a goblet, and other items blocked from my vantage point.

Taking the lead from the cloaked couple, the four non Wiccans stood to the left of the table. Shannon appeared at the garden entrance wearing an emerald green robe as she walked forward barefooted. Roisin followed her mother. Her robe was royal purple. She was also barefoot. Desmond was dressed in an all black robe, and like the others, shoeless. The three went to the right of the table, Lugh trotted to his family, ignoring everyone else, and laid in front of the table.

"I want to welcome and cast blessings on each of you for joining us in our time of transition," Shannon said in a voice stronger than earlier.

Roisin stepped forward and speaking softly but with confidence said, "Most of you have never been to a Wiccan ritual. Allow me to explain." She moved to the table then rested her hand gently on the top. "This is the altar. On it, we have items representing the elements, each meaningful in its own way; also the reason we are here today, my dad." Her voice trailed off. Lugh nuzzled against her foot. The young lady looked at Lugh, smiled, then continued, "During our ritual, we ask you to let the moment into your soul." Roisin took a step back next to her brother.

Shannon stepped forward. "I ask everyone to form a semi circle in front of the altar. Desmond, Roisin, Darrin and I will be lighting the candles at the four points around the circle representing north, south, east, west."

I hadn't noticed the large white candles on stands around the perimeter of the garden, thinking it strange since they were some of the largest I'd seen. We formed the semi circle as the four went to their candle saying something I couldn't make out, then lit the wicks. Darrin and the kids joined the circle as Shannon walked to the table and lit a candle on each side of the altar.

"Please join hands to make our circle complete so we can honor Mike." Shannon's voice cracked as her daughter's had. Lugh nuzzled against her foot as he had with Roisin.

We joined hands. I hated to admit I was thankful I was between Charles and Burl. I wasn't in a hurry to see if mini Ozzy Osbourne felt as cold as he looked.

Shannon lifted a large dagger from the altar and held it in her outstretched hand. Slowly turning in a circle, she placed the dagger down. She chanted and said what sounded like a prayer. The words were loud enough but I couldn't make them out. Music was playing in the background. I hadn't noticed when it began. It was both haunting and soothing.

Shannon then turned to us asking if anyone wanted to say final words or pay their last respects.

Burl cleared his throat. Shannon's hand extended. "Burl, please come forward."

He stepped close to the widow and said, "Sister Shannon, I want to say what an honor it was getting to know Brother Mike. He was truly a great and loving man who thought the world of his family. I'm a better man for knowing him."

"Blessed be." Shannon said as she squeezed Burl's arm as he returned to the chain. She turned to her daughter. "Roisin, do you wish to speak?"

The young lady stepped forward. In a low voice, said, "I will miss you, Dad. I know you are with us and this is a new adventure for you. I only wish the adventure here could have lasted longer." Tears streamed down her cheeks, but she held her head high.

Shannon said, "Blessed be, my little nymph. Desmond, want to say something?"

Desmond stood at the other end of the circle from me and shook his head but didn't make a sound.

Shannon turned to the altar and spoke in what I assumed to be Gaelic as she bent to place her forehead on the urn. She then stood, reached for the dagger, walked to each of the four large candles, and with the blade snuffed out the flames. She returned to the altar and said, "The circle is broken. Mingle and be merry."

Shannon asked Desmond, Stormy, and Darrin to help with refreshments.

Charles moved toward the altar, I assumed to get a better look. Knowing Charles the way I did, I went with him to make sure he remained toad free. About three feet from his destination, a loud growl stopped us in our tracks. Lugh was again protecting his master.

"Lugh, you know they mean no harm," Roisin said, as she moved beside Charles then led us closer to the altar.

"Interesting service," Charles said, then reached out to the altar.

Roisin grabbed his hand before it touched anything. "Only family can touch. It's still a sacred place. We will allow the candles on the altar to burn. When they are finished, this part of the ritual will be completed."

I said, "Roisin, I'd like to introduce Charles, my best friend."

She let go of Charles's hand, smiled, and said, "So nice to meet you, Mr. Charles. Mom and Lugh told me good things about you."

Charles said, "Roisin, it's a pleasure meeting you. I'm terribly sorry about your loss."

She lowered her head before saying, "Thank you."

"May I ask a question?"

"Of course."

"What happens if wind blows out the candles? Do you relight them?"

"Mr. Charles, they will not be blown out or desecrated by rain. The Goddess does not allow that during this most sacred ritual."

"Are you going to bury the ashes or scatter them?" Charles asked since he has no brakes on his question machine.

"On Halloween, the family only will complete the ritual by scattering Dad's ashes. All Hallows Eve is our most sacred holiday where we honor our departed loved ones. It's the perfect day for us to complete the ritual."

Charles and I silently gazed at the items on the table, before Roisin added, "Mr. Chris, Mr. Charles, may I ask something?"

"Of course, Roisin," Charles said in a soft voice. "What do—"

She looked around before saying, "Not here. Please follow me to my fairy garden."

Burl apparently noticed that his name wasn't mentioned. He hugged her and said, "Roisin, I shall speak to your mother and brother."

Charles and I followed her to the far side of the house. The side yard was small but quaint and childlike. There were honeysuckle vines hanging from a trellis, a small wrought iron bench below a window, and what appeared to be a tiny village made of mushroom houses and small fairy figurines. A small dragonfly fountain added to the mystical setting.

"This is lovely. Your own little world," Charles said, as he patted the young girl on the arm.

She smiled. "Mom says it's my Zen place."

I hesitated while trying to find the right words to add.

Before I spoke and surprisingly before Charles could speak, Roisin pointed to a window above the bench. "That's Dad's office. It was here where I heard Dad talking to someone on the phone. He seemed, umm, what's the word, umm, distressed. Most days he has the window open so he can hear the fountain. It relaxes him." She looked at the fountain. "Mom says it will always bring him peace."

"Your mom's a wise lady," Charles said as he looked toward the window. "Do you know who he was speaking to?"

"Think his name was Todd."

My turn. "Roisin, did your dad say anything that might help figure out who Todd was talking about?"

"Dad said anyone can be deadly when cornered. He suggested Todd meet dad in person. That is all I remember. Does that help?"

Charles gave Roisin a hug, "Helps a lot."

I remembered something Nate Davis had shared. "Roisin, do you remember if your dad said anything about blackmail when he was talking to Todd?"

She looked back at the window. "Mr. Chris, I'm not familiar with that word."

I keep forgetting she's only eleven. "Roisin, it means someone demands payment from another person because he knows something and if he gets the money, he won't tell what he knows. It's illegal." I realized that was oversimplifying blackmail, but it was the best I could do on the spur of the moment.

She rubbed her chin. "Oh, okay. Thanks for enlightening me." She shook her head. "I don't recall dad saying anything like that. Sorry."

Charles said, "That's okay. You've been helpful. Let's join the others."

"Roisin," I said, "why did you want to share that information about the phone call?"

She stopped and looked toward the bench. "Mr. Chris, I have faith that you, you too, Mr. Charles, will catch the person that took dad away from the adventure he was sharing with me."

I said, "I don't—"

Charles interrupted, "Roisin, we will."

Thanks, Charles.

As we walked to the group gathered around a table with

refreshments, someone caught my eye although my view was partially blocked by the shrubbery near the drive. I couldn't swear to it, but it appeared to be a woman with long blond hair getting into a pickup truck. By the time I moved to get a better view, the truck had disappeared around the corner.

Chapter Twenty-Six

When I answered the phone early the next morning, Cindy LaMond greeted me with, "I'm disappointed in you,"

"Why?" A logical question, I thought.

"It's almost three days since you found Mike Stone's body, and you haven't called to harass me about what else I learned from the Stone family or what Detective Adair discovered from his interviews."

"Sorry to disappoint you. What did you and Adair learn?"

"That's more like Chris Landrum, the one taking nosy lessons from Charles. The answers to your questions along with my check for breakfast can be found at the Dog."

"You there now?"

"Yep, getting ready to order a second breakfast. Hurry, or I'm going to add lunch to go."

"On my way."

I'm certain she would have said *Great. I look forward to seeing you.* It must've slipped her mind. She'd hung up.

A quick look out the window told me it was a clear, sunny day, so I walked instead of driving to my go to breakfast spot. Ten minutes later, I found the Chief at a table along the side wall. She may've been serious about ordering a second breakfast. Two plates, one empty, one with an order of bacon and eggs were in front of her.

She nodded toward the chair across from her and said, "In the nick of time. Lori said she'd save room on your check so you could order something."

As if on cue, Lori, one of the Dog's college age servers, was at the table setting a mug of coffee in front of me.

Cindy said, "He wants French toast."

Lori glanced at me, I shrugged, and she headed to put in my order. I wasn't certain if it was good or bad when the Chief of Police knows what I ordered for breakfast nearly every time I was here.

"Morning, Cindy," I said interjecting civility to the conversation.

She stuffed a bite of egg in her mouth, washed it down with coffee, and said, "Desmond Stone told Detective Adair he went to the store with his Dad. Came home and had on earphones and playing music, or that's what Adair called the screaming hyenas the kid was listening to."

Yes, my attempt at civility had failed.

"Go on."

"The Goth witch claimed he didn't know anything was wrong until stormtrooper cops did what stormtroopers do and stormed in his room and pointed their guns in his face." She sighed. "Chris, since I was half the stormtrooper force, I'll admit, I did have my firearm drawn. Had no idea who or what I'd find in the house, but never pointed my weapon at young Mr. Stone. He, Desmond, not Detective Adair, then went on a rant about the police state not having respect for the privacy of law abiding citizens in their own homes."

"Did Adair find or hear anything indicating Desmond had anything to do with his father's death?"

"Not really. He attributed most of Desmond's bluster to him being traumatized by learning of the death. Regardless of his hostile attitude, it had to be horrible learning his father was killed a few yards from where Desmond was enjoying stuff he calls music."

"Did Desmond say anything about his father talking to Todd Lee or anything that would tie the two together?"

"If he did, Adair didn't share it."

"What's your gut reaction to Desmond?"

"I'm no shrink, but it seems he's a scared kid hiding behind his Goth appearance and attitude."

"You may not have the degrees, but you're one of the most perceptive people I know."

"Suck up all you want, but you're still buying breakfast, correction, breakfasts."

"Never doubted it. Did Adair learn anything new or important from Shannon or Roisin?"

She took another bite of my purchase, then said, "No. As you know, they were more shook than anything. If he learned more, he didn't think it was important enough to share."

"Did either of them say anything about Mike's contacts with Todd Lee?"

"They knew he'd been in contact, assumed it was about legal issues Lee was having."

I shared what Roisin had said at the ceremony about her dad's demeanor change after talking on the phone.

"When was I going to hear about this?"

"Cindy, it was yesterday and here we are today with me telling you."

She exhaled, rolled her eyes, took another sip of coffee, before saying, "Anything else you're holding back?"

Might as well get it over with, especially since we're in a public place with witnesses in case she tried to shoot me.

"Chief, when you were in Stone's house, did you notice a small round table in a room off the entry?"

"I was there to see if a killer was lurking, not inventorying furniture."

"When Preacher Burl and I were there the first time there were various tools and other items on the small table, among them, an ice pick."

My hands gripped the table waiting for the explosion.

"Crap on a cucumber, Chris. You saw an ice pick like the thing that killed Todd Lee?"

This was a good time to use Charles's logic. "Yes, but there's no reason to think it was the murder weapon. At one time, about every house over here had an ice pick."

"At one time, every house had an outhouse. At one time, there were Bohicket Indians roaming this island instead of vacationers. At one time, there—"

"Got it. I'm simply saying an ice pick is a common tool."

"Not common as a murder weapon, is it?"

"I don't think—"

She waved a hand in my face. "Enough. Did you see it yesterday when you were there for the funeral?"

"We didn't go in the house."

"After I finish this breakfast, order lunch for Larry, get him some dessert as a bonus, and heck, order some for me as well, I'll pay a visit to the Stones to see if they have any murder weapons laying around."

"Good police work, Chief." I smiled, hoping for a similar response.

That was too much to hope for. She shook her head, frowned, and said, "I feel sorry for them."

"Why?"

"Don't know much about the Wiccan religion, hell's bells, I don't know much about most religions, but what I do know is there's a lot of hate, distrust, and confusion about Wiccan. From what little I know about the Stone family, they seem like good folks. They haven't been trouble to anyone I know."

"Except one of them may be a killer?" I added with a smile. Again, an attempt to reduce Cindy's ire.

"That would shoot a hole in my *good folks*' theory, but that's not my point."

"What's your point?"

"We've received calls, anonymous, of course, claiming the witches on East Huron Avenue are sacrificing animals in their back yard. People are afraid their precious pets will be next. One lady called to say she's afraid for her granddaughter, afraid the witches will sacrifice her. You know about the broom on the porch and the nasty note with it, but you probably don't know about the letter, unsigned, of course, accusing the Stones of casting a spell and turning the writer's husband into a turnip."

I smiled.

"Chris, I'm serious."

"Okay, I'll remember the next time I eat a turnip it may be someone's husband."

Cindy forced back a smile and repeated. "I'm serious."

"Cindy, I know. Remember, I was there yesterday for a funeral. I've been to several funerals over the years, several religions. Mike's was unique, but everything said and done made sense."

She looked at her watch. "I understand. I simply wanted you to know, not all people's impressions of witchcraft are based on *Bewitched*. There's an overabundance of hostility and fear out there."

"Thanks for sharing."

"Chris, I need to meet with the mayor. If I believed any of the stories I've been hearing, I'd ask Shannon to cast a spell on him, maybe turn him into an eggplant." She looked around. "You didn't hear that."

I smiled.

"Thanks for the information about the ice pick. Maybe the next clue you get, you can share it with me the same century."

"Good luck meeting with the mayor and ice pick hunting. One more thing, Cindy, did Adair have anything new to report on Jeff Hildebrand?"

"Nope."

"Nothing to tie him to the murder other than what he said about removing his and Lee's possessions from the haunted house?"

"Is there some reason you didn't think *nope* covered that?"

I smiled. "Nope."

"Adair didn't tell me, but one of my officers saw Hildebrand back on our quaint little island."

"Where's he staying?"

"No idea."

"That helps."

"Nope," she said, smiled, and headed to the door, before

adding, "Thanks for the breakfasts, Larry's lunch, and two desserts."

Chapter Twenty-Seven

Lousy October weather had finally arrived, so the next morning was spent piddling around the house. The last several weeks had been a roller coaster, so self isolation was the plan of the day.

After an attempt at cleaning house, I decided getting out for a late lunch would beat isolation. I was sitting in the car in my driveway realizing I had no real plan on where I was going. Minutes later, I found myself parked in front of Cal's, telling myself my subconscious had made a wise decision. What could beat good country music from Cal's antique Wurlitzer, a heart unhealthy cheeseburger, and listening to Cal's stories about the past?

I was greeted by the Statler Brothers on the jukebox singing "The Class of '57" with Cal harmonizing with the quartet while drying a glass with an orange and black bar towel. I took the table closest to the bar when he noticed me and headed my way during the song's last verse. He plopped down across from me.

"How's Chris?"

"Good, and you?"

"Had to beat customers away with a two-by-four. You know how busy this time of year is." Cal smiled as he spread his arms gesturing around the near empty room.

I smiled. "That couple at the bar and the folks at those two tables make it look like you might be over capacity. The fire marshal might come a callin' any minute."

"Been working on your sarcasm?"

"Nope, comes naturally. Besides, you started it."

"Whatever. What can I get you?"

"Martini and a club sandwich."

Cal stood, patted me on the shoulder. "Wine and cheeseburger coming right up," he said before heading to the kitchen.

I scanned the bar and was amazed how businesses on Folly made a profit during the winter months. There are always small groups of vacationers around, and locals venture out more during the slow season, but regardless, business was anything but brisk. I didn't recognize any of today's patrons.

It wasn't long before Cal returned with two cheeseburgers, one beer, and my wine.

"Figure you could use some company since Charles ain't here. You mind?"

"Not at all. You need to get some rest before the next big wave of customers arrives."

"Sarcasm! I'd write a song about you and use it, but it's hard for this old crooner finding words to rhyme with sarcasm." He smiled, pulled out the chair, then we toasted our good fortune and started on the closest menu item he had to a club sandwich.

Cal leaned back in his chair, looked around the far from capacity crowd, and said, "Seems several people haven't been having good fortune as of late. Two murders on our little island, and you're in the middle of both." Cal chuckled. "No surprise there."

"Not in the middle," I said, then sipped my drink while waiting for what might come next.

"Chris, I've been going around our island for months, heck, years, and haven't come across one dead body. You've gone and found two this month. Sounds like you're in the middle to me."

"Cal, it's a gift."

"Sarcasm. Your good buddy Charles was in last night telling me more than I wanted to know about the murders and how you two are on the trail of the killer or killers."

"Yes, I've found two unfortunate souls, but that doesn't mean I'm involved in doing anything about it."

Cal smiled. "If you say so. All I know is with you and Charles on the case, a killer will be off the streets soon." Cal raised his beer in my direction before finishing it off.

I sighed and said, "I'm sure the authorities can handle homicides much better than Charles and I."

"If you say so," he repeated. "I do have someone you might like to talk to about at least one of the murders." Cal's sly grin beamed from under the Stetson.

"Who?"

"Jeff Hildebrand. He's around here somewhere. I'm having him help out. Nothing much, just some chores to earn a few bucks, plus meals."

"How long has he been here?"

"Since the fuzz let him go. Found him walking down

Folly Road during that nasty thunderstorm the other day. Gave him a lift."

"Known him long?"

"Yeah, since way back when I saw him in the storm. The boy was soaked. Gave him a ride back here figuring I could help the guy out. I know what it's like being down on your luck. Been there a time or two myself."

"I'd like to talk to him if you don't think he'd mind."

Cal smiled. "Not getting involved?"

"Curious."

Cal's smile turned into a laugh. "I'm sure he wouldn't mind. Let me see where he is."

Funny how things work out. I was going to mind my own business today and not seek anyone to do a Charles interrogation on and look what fell into my lap. I also wondered why Cal hadn't introduced Charles to Jeff last night, but then again Cal's smart so there must've been a good reason.

Cal returned from the kitchen followed by a man wearing black jeans and a long sleeve T shirt with Led Zeppelin on the front. He was my height, long brown and graying hair in a ponytail and younger by a decade or more.

"Jeff this is Chris Landrum. Chris, Jeff Hildebrand."

I stood to shake Jeff's hand. "Nice to meet you, Jeff."

"You a cop, a cop?" He held his hand down to his side.

"No."

Jeff smiled and extended his hand for the greeting. Cal pointed to the chair he'd occupied and told Jeff to have a seat, said he had to take care of some business, and there was no rush for Jeff to get back to work. Jeff slowly lowered himself in the chair.

He looked everywhere but at me and said, "Sorry about

the cop comment. I'm a little gun shy. Cal said you're okay and I should answer your questions about Todd, about Todd." Jeff's eyes continued darting around the room like he was looking for eavesdroppers, or maybe cops.

"Kind of him, I'm looking into some things going on the last couple of weeks. It started with Todd Lee's murder."

Jeff finally made eye contact. "I didn't kill him if that's where you're headed."

"Didn't think you did, Jeff. I know the police picked you up for tampering with physical evidence."

I wasn't sure if I thought Jeff didn't kill Todd, but it seemed to be the right thing to say to keep him talking.

"That's what they got me for. Umm, I admitted it, but that's all I did, all I did." He shook his head.

"Tell me what you know about Todd and what you think happened?"

Jeff stared at the table. I looked around the room and noticed ours was now the only occupied table. The couple at the bar were laughing, and Cal was singing along with the jukebox playing Hank Williams Sr's hit "Lovesick Blues." He caught my glance, so I motioned for a refill. He was quick bringing a glass of wine for me and a beer for Jeff. Only then did Jeff look up from the table, appearing puzzled at seeing Cal and the beer.

"Jeff," Cal said, "you need the drink. Don't worry about anything." Cal patted him on the back and headed to the bar.

Jeff took a sip, then looked at me. "I don't know much about Todd, then again, not sure if anyone knew much about the guy. He had an attitude, thought he was always right, always right. Had a chip on his shoulder the size of Cal's Stetson."

"That's what I heard. Do you know why he was on Folly or who might've wanted him dead?"

"Why are any of us here? He came from Savannah, wanted to be near the beach, he said, but didn't strike me as a sun worshiper. Besides, there're beaches closer to where he came from than having to come this far, this far." Jeff paused, and took a long draw of beer, then continued, "He told me when he was on his last job he found out something that'd make him a lot of money if he played his cards right."

"Did he elaborate?"

He shook his head. "Said people with businesses should pay more attention to the little people and not look over them like they're equipment because those little people see everything."

"Know what business he was talking about or who the people were?"

"No, that was the first night we stayed in the haunted house. Probably in construction since that's what he was doing here." He looked around the room, took a sip, then continued, "He seemed determined to get his money, but things changed."

"How?"

"I didn't see Todd for a couple of days, I then ran into him late one night on my way to the house where he was just standing outside by the bushes looking scared."

"Anyone else around?"

"Not that I saw. The haunted house was closed; the crew was gone for the night. I made a joke about him fearing a ghost, a ghost. Wanted to lighten his mood, you know."

"Did it?"

"Not a bit. He said something about the living are the scary ones, not the dead."

"Did you two spend that night in the house?"

"Yeah, it was too cold to be out and looked like rain. We talked most of the night about life and other stuff but nothing about what scared him or his big windfall. Was like he was avoiding his favorite subject, money."

"Sounds like something was bothering him," I said, attempting to get more without sounding pushy.

"That was our last night there. The next day I met a guy at the hardware store. He needed help building a deck. I offered to help for some cash. Job took three days and he let me stay in his garage." Jeff took another drink of beer. "I finally had some cash in my pocket, so I went back to the house to tell Todd we should spend a couple of nights at a hotel. I never felt good about sneaking in someone else's place." He took a deep breath, closed his eyes, his hand balled into a fist. "That's when I found him, found him."

"That must've been horrible."

"I never seen a dead body before. He was in the kitchen. I dragged him to the pantry and closed the door." Jeff's hands were shaking.

"Why the pantry?"

He shook his head. "I didn't want some crewmember or especially some youngster going through the haunted house finding him on the kitchen floor. That could mess up some kid. I grabbed all our stuff and left so no one would know we'd been staying there."

"Okay," I said, not sure what else to say to this man who was visibly shaken about the experience.

I didn't have to say anything. He offered, "I didn't go to

the cops because, well, I'm no angel. I just wanted to forget everything."

"I understand. After you found him, did you see anyone around the house?"

"Didn't see anyone but heard something in the front of the house, But there was no way I was going to the room with the coffin. All I wanted to do was grab our things and get the hell out of there."

"I don't blame you."

He looked at his trembling hands. "Chris, I wasn't always like this. Sometimes life keeps knocking you down. I'm trying to get back on my feet. You've got to believe me. I'd never hurt anyone, anyone."

"Jeff, it sounds like you're taking a good first step, Cal's a great guy to have in your corner. Thanks for sharing. It was helpful."

Jeff looked around to make sure no one was nearby and said, "If you want it, I still got Todd's stuff."

"The police didn't get it from you?"

He shook his head. "Told them I threw it in a dumpster, just didn't feel right handing over a man's whole life to someone who was just doing a job."

"Do you have his things here?"

"I'm not going all over Folly with a dead man's gear. I can get it to you in a couple of days if you want."

"Jeff, that'd be great."

He stood. "I'll have Cal get ahold of you when I get Todd's things." He attempted a smile. "Thanks for the talk. Made me feel better."

He left the table and disappeared into the kitchen. I was left alone in the bar wondering what I'd agreed to. Does this make me an accomplice to withholding evidence? Cal was nowhere in sight, so I left money on the table to cover my bill and headed to the door to contemplate what to do next and if I should wait to call Charles later or get it over with now.

The sound of Hank Locklin singing "Please Help Me I'm Falling" followed me out.

Chapter Twenty-Eight

Yesterday's cold, dreary weather that'd limited my activities to a trip to Cal's had made way for temperatures in the low seventies and a clear blue sky. After grabbing a cup of coffee from Bert's, I made my way to the diamond shaped upper level of the Folly Pier. My conversation with Jeff Hildebrand reinforced my belief that he wasn't responsible for Todd Lee's death and that Lee had sights on blackmailing someone. Who and why remained unanswered.

Prior to meeting Hildebrand, my talk with Cindy hadn't revealed anything I didn't know or suspect. At least, she'd check on the ice pick at the Stone's house. While I couldn't imagine any of the Stones killing the family's patriarch, I wasn't as certain about one of them not stabbing Todd Lee. Desmond would be my prime suspect if I had to limit it to a member of the family. Was that simply because of his demeanor, his appearance, his constant scowl, or his apparent dislike for most anyone I'd seen him interact with?

I didn't get to analyze the teenager deeper. I heard

Charles's cane tapping on the steps to the upper level before I saw him.

He was out of breath as he reached the top step, but it didn't stop him from saying, "Knew you'd be here."

He was wearing a long sleeve red sweatshirt with Nebraska on the front, jeans with a tear in each knee, a Tilley, and tennis shoes.

"How?"

"I'm guessin' that's not an Indian greeting. I knew you'd be here because you're not at the Dog, not at your house, not at Loggerhead's, not at the Tides, so where else would you be but here?"

That'll teach me to ask.

He plopped down beside me, took two deep breaths, then said, "Herbie Husker."

"Who's Herbie Husker," I said, regretting it before it was out of my mouth.

He pointed to the front of his sweatshirt. "University of Nebraska's mascot, duh."

"You were looking for me to share that?"

"Nope. Wanted you to experience a teaching moment."

"Then why did—"

"Speaking of trivia," he interrupted, "that reminds me. Did you know Skittles are the number one Halloween candy? They're more popular than M&M's, Snickers, and Reese's Cups. Can you believe that?"

"Wow," I said, with a sugary bite of sarcasm, "two teaching moments in one morning. What did I do to deserve such enlightenment?"

"You making fun of me?"

"Yep. Now, why did you go all over town looking for me?"

"I went to the Dog and Lori told me you'd been there yesterday meeting with the Chief. I figured she told you something you'd want to share, but since you didn't call, I knew your phone must be busted. I ate breakfast so I'd have the energy to find you, then here I am."

"You could've called."

"Wouldn't have done any good if your phone's busted. Besides, our detecting skills work best when we're together."

For the three-thousandth time I chose not to remind him we weren't detectives. "Would you like to know what Cindy told me?"

"Yes."

"Nothing."

"Nothing, what?"

"Chief LaMond didn't tell me anything I didn't know or suspect."

"I looked all over town for you for that?"

"Yep."

"Really, she told you nothing new?"

"Correct." I smiled. "Want to hear who I met yesterday"

"Did he or she confess to killing both men?"

"Don't think so."

"Then who?"

"Jeff Hildebrand."

Charles nearly fell off the bench. "When were you going to tell me?"

"Now," I said and smiled once more, hoping to prevent a tirade.

He frowned. "Chris, you met the killer and didn't think it was important enough to tell me until now?"

Yes, I knew I'd regret not calling him yesterday. "Charles, I don't think he's the killer." I then shared as much as I could remember about my conversation with Jeff.

Charles pouted through me telling him and asked a minimal number of questions—minimal for Charles. He then said, "Chris, that makes all of it as clear as day. Cindy hasn't figured it out. The hotshot Sheriff's Office detective is sitting on his hands doing nothing. If Hildebrand didn't do it, it's up to us to find the killer. Clear as day."

"And how are we going to do that?"

"Herbert Hoover said, 'A good many things go around in the dark besides Santa Claus.'"

"Other than mixing holidays, what's that have to do with anything?"

"The answer is right there in the dark waiting for us to figure it out. See, that's why we're meeting. Who are the suspects?"

I'm glad it made sense to one of us. I've learned over the years, moving quickly past something Charles says, is often the best route to sanity. This is one of those times.

I said, "We suspect Todd Lee was blackmailing someone, and if Jeff Hildebrand is right, it's someone Lee met before he got to Folly."

"Good, then it's Fred Robinson."

"Why?"

"Todd Lee lived in Savannah before moving here. Fred and, umm, Mrs. Fred also lived there."

"Erika."

"Okay, Fred and Erika. There you go, one of them did it. Case closed. Go ahead, call Cindy with the good news."

"Charles, other than Fred being a jerk, what reason would he or his wife have for killing Lee?"

"If I knew that, I'd call Cindy myself. If Lee was blackmailing Fred, there must've been a good reason. Jerks do jerky things. Lee could've known about some of them."

I realized I hadn't told Charles about seeing the blond haired woman at Mike's funeral. I moved his cane, aka weapon, out of his reach and shared what I'd seen.

He opened his mouth, closed it, rolled his eyes, then said, "You let me accuse the dentist and his wife when you knew the killer was Bri Rice?"

"Charles, I don't know that."

"Then why was she there?"

"First, I'm not certain it was her, and if it was, she could've been walking in the neighborhood, not there for the funeral."

"I have better odds of being elected President than she had for *walking in the neighborhood*." He snapped his fingers. "Didn't Hildebrand say Lee was blackmailing someone about something that happened before they got here?"

"Yes."

"Bri knew Lee when they were in Charleston before they got here. See, more proof she killed him."

I reminded him it was the same argument he used moments earlier when he was accusing one of the Robinsons.

"Yes, but they weren't sneaking around the Stone's house at the funeral."

"We also need to consider Desmond as a suspect."

"Because of the ice pick?"

"Yes," I said, "and because he was at the house when his dad was killed. He had opportunity and knew Shannon and Roisin were in Charleston."

"What's his motive?"

"Charles, I don't know. I don't want it to be him, but the

ice pick and proximity to Mike's death have to be considered."

"But what about Lee blackmailing someone?"

"Even if he was, it may not have had anything to do with his murder."

"Where does that leave us?"

I smiled. "Enjoying a beautiful October day."

"While being confused about the murder, murders."

"Yes."

Chapter Twenty-Nine

Other than concluding Todd Lee was blackmailing someone and was killed because of it, our suspect list was weak at best. On that unsatisfying analysis, Charles announced he needed to make three deliveries for Dude and left me on the Pier. I wasn't ready to let the pleasant day go to waste, so I headed east on the beach for some much-needed exercise, not quite on the level of going to the gym, but that was never going to happen.

I looked down the shoreline and the only living things I saw were sandpipers running to then scampering back from water's edge. The little birds reminded me of kids rushing to go in the ocean but as soon as a wave greeted them, they'd scamper back to their parents.

I was so entertained by the birds' antics I wasn't aware of someone behind me until I heard,

"Crazy, aren't they?"

I jumped and twisted around to see what kind of goblin

had followed me. There was no goblin, but a witch in the form of Desmond—dark, wicked Desmond.

"You surprised me," I said, trying to act more composed than I felt.

"Sorry, Mr. Landrum." Desmond smirked, but lowered his head.

"I didn't see anyone around."

"I was behind the dunes when you came down from the Pier. Been waiting for you to finish talking to the cane guy."

That didn't sound encouraging. I have a potential killer hiding out, waiting for me to be alone, then following me to where no one could hear me call for help. My internal monologue was still playing as I looked at Desmond, then around to see if I could make a quick exit.

"Mr. Landrum, sorry I startled you," he said as he looked me in my eyes. "I need to talk to you."

For the first time, I saw something less frightening from the boy in black.

"Want to go somewhere where we can sit and talk?"

He moved closer and looked around. "I'd rather talk here."

"Okay, what's on your mind?"

"My sister likes you. Lugh trusts you. That preacher brought you to us, and he thinks good of you. I figured you're the best person to talk to."

"Roisin is a special young lady." I smiled. "Lugh hasn't eaten me yet, so I guess we're okay."

The prince of darkness returned my smile. For the first time, I didn't feel like I was about to meet Todd Lee in the hereafter.

His smile faded. "Mr. Landrum, I'm not evil. I didn't kill

Dad or the stiff in the haunted house." He shrugged. "Maybe I'm different, but I'm not a monster."

"Desmond, I've never said you killed anyone."

"Bet you thought it." His head lowered as he slowly shook it. "It's okay if you did. Everyone else does."

"I have questions, not accusations. Sadly, many people accuse before getting the facts."

He gave a muted grin. "That means the world's full of those people."

"I've met plenty."

He kicked the sand and stared at the horizon. "People think because I have a different way of living, different clothes, different beliefs that I must be evil. My family had some issues in Minnesota but there are a lot more here. The Twin Cities has a larger Wiccan community with more tolerance."

"I bet once people get to know you and your family, feelings will be different. You have to give them a chance to see the real person, not a disguise."

He looked at his foot kicking more sand. "Not going to change who I am to suit people." He turned his gaze to me. "I get your point. Will sort of work on it."

"Desmond, you didn't track me down for advice. What's on your mind?"

He nodded. "Mr. Landrum, umm, I picked up an ice pick from the yard behind the haunted house after Roisin and I went through it."

"The night after Todd Lee was killed?"

"Yeah, the ice pick is a cool old tool. I collect old tools and knives. They're from a simpler time before we had all the electronic stuff. Anyway, I didn't give it a second thought. I find old stuff laying around all the time." He took a deep breath, then continued, "Took it home, didn't know it was used to kill someone." He sighed. "Who ever heard of getting stabbed with an ice pick?"

"True," I said, "never heard of it until the police said Mr. Lee was stabbed with one. Did Roisin or your mom know you found it?"

"No," he said and smiled. "Thought it was a guy thing." His smile disappeared. "After Dad was killed, the police came to the house and took it. So, here I am with maybe the murder weapon. I was home when you found Dad. Mr. Landrum, all I need is to be around one more dead dude and it's three strikes and I'm out. I'll be up a creek."

"Pretty sure that's not how it works, but I understand it doesn't look good. Did you tell the police where you got the ice pick?"

"A hundred times. Had to tell it to the Folly Chief, then to that detective from the Sheriff's Office, then write it all down like it was a school assignment. Then, Mr. Landrum, after all that, the Folly woman took me to the haunted house. I had to show her exactly where I found it." He sighed. "A pain in the, umm, butt, if you ask me."

"That could help them catch the killer."

"Whatever."

I didn't think it was a good time to tell him I was the one who told the police the potential murder weapon was in his house.

He was more relaxed the longer the conversation went on. I began to see him as a young man playing a role to keep out the world. Self isolation was seldom a good thing, but if his way of life was ridiculed, it didn't leave many options, especially for a sixteen-year-old.

"I loved dad. We had our differences, but he was my hero, our family rock."

"All boys have differences with their dads."

"He thought I should be myself and quit putting on the Grim Reaper vibe. He called me out on it, sort of like you just did. Guess it's from the old person playbook."

I smiled. "I'd prefer to say it's from experience. Desmond, does anything stand out to you from the day your dad died?"

He looked out to sea again, then said, "I went to the grocery with him. We were having one of our arguments. When we got home, I went to my room, turned up the volume on my headsets to tune the world out. That always ticks him off, says the noise will hurt my ears."

"Anything unusual happen when you were at the store? Did your Dad talk to anyone?"

"He just talked, sort of yelled at me. To be honest, our fight started when we were shopping." Desmond picked up a shell and threw it in the surf. "I was being a brat about Dad's job. Told him he needed to spend more time with us. Told him he was letting some stupid stiff in a haunted house ruin his time at home."

"You brought up Todd Lee?"

"Dad was supposed to be off work getting ready for Halloween, but he needed to meet with you first. Like I said, I was being a brat. Dad always put Mom, me, and Roisin first."

"He told you he was going to meet me?"

"Yeah, he told me he'd talked to you once but needed to meet you again that afternoon, something about the stiff. Said once it was done, he'd be free to plan for the holiday."

"Did anyone hear your conversation?"

"Could have, we weren't whispering. Actually, I was sort of yelling." He shook his head. "Stupid me, yelling in the grocery store. I know better; honest I do. Think it startled someone in the next row."

"Why do you think that?"

"Guess I scared her because she dropped a jar then left in a hurry." He kicked sand as he told me.

"Did you see her?"

"No."

"How do you know it was a woman?"

"A cart with food in it was still in the row beside a busted jar of pickles."

"That made you think it was a woman?"

He rubbed his eyes. "Not the cart. Think I know it was a lady because men don't wear perfume. Smelled it strong."

"Desmond, anything else stand out about that morning."

"Nope, we left the store and headed home. Was raining hard. We were still arguing but dad seemed distracted. Could've been the hard rain because he kept watching the mirrors like he was worried someone might run into the back of the car."

"Did you go inside when you got home, or did you help carry the groceries?"

"Went inside. dad was still in the car when I stomped off to the house."

"Why did he stay in the car?"

"Don't know. I was pissed and didn't care." He sighed then avoided eye contact. "Mr. Landrum, the last thing I said to my dad was mean. How do I go on? No matter what I do now, I'll never feel his arms around me telling me it'll be okay."

"Desmond, your Dad knows you were just being a teenager. It was nothing you two wouldn't have worked out."

"Mr. Landrum, if I stayed outside to help with the groceries, he'd still be alive. My family blames me for his death. So do I." Tears streamed down his face making him look like a sad goth clown.

"That's not true. Your family loves you and wants nothing more than to help you through this horrible time. As far as stopping your Dad from being killed, you couldn't have stopped it. If not then, whoever did it, would've tried again."

He wiped tears from his face and attempted a weak smile. "Roisin is right. You're a good soul to talk to. Hope she's right about the other thing."

"Other thing?"

"She said you'll find who killed Dad and even the stiff, umm, Mr. Lee."

"I'm not sure why she said that, but I'll help with anything I can."

"She is an old soul and knows things, except about the Bermuda Triangle." He pointed to the ocean and his vision of where the Triangle is located.

"Young man, you're more like your father than you know. He told me the same thing about Roisin the first time I talked to him."

Desmond smiled and looked at the churning sea which seemed to get rougher since we'd been standing here. A dense fog enveloped the end of the Pier.

"Thanks, Mr. Landrum. I need to get home. May talk to you later if that's okay."

I told him any time and watched the not so scary Ozzy

Osbourne looking young man disappear in the fog as it rolled in from the ocean. Our suspect list was now shortened by one.

I headed home before Desmond's Bermuda Triangle fog took me away. His story kept bouncing around in my head. He'd mentioned a woman. That would knock our suspects down to half the population but in fact not a huge help since the unanswered questions keep piling up. Another brain worm weaseled its way into my head as I reached my door. Desmond said his Dad had mentioned talking to me once about Todd Lee. Did the mystery woman hear Desmond and Mike's conversation?

It was enough to make me look over my shoulder before opening the door.

Chapter Thirty

I was awakened the next morning by heavy rain pounding my metal roof and a headache pounding my brain. *Not the most pleasant way to begin the day*, I thought as I padded to the kitchen to start my Mr. Coffee machine and search for a bottle of ibuprofen. Thirty minutes later, coffee had begun to do its thing while the wonder drug had begun attacking the headache. Neither coffee nor ibuprofen had lessened the amount of rain covering my island home, so I decided it would be the perfect day to stay indoors, a decision reinforced when I found a three day old box of powdered sugar covered donuts in the cabinet. A breakfast gift from the heavens.

A television commercial plugging a pop up Halloween store reminded me the holiday was rapidly approaching. Instead of the commercial inspiring me to visit the store to buy costumes, pumpkin carving kits, or skull shaped candy bowls, it made me think about Desmond and the ice pick he claimed he found in the haunted house's yard the day after Todd Lee had taken his last breath.

The ringing phone interrupted my less than helpful thoughts.

"Hey, pard, here's a heads up."

Cal had caught some of my friends irritating habit of beginning phone conversations by skipping civil phone etiquette openings.

"Morning, Cal."

"Yeah, okay. Want the heads up or not?"

"Cal, what's the heads up?"

"That's better, pard. Jeff asked me to tell you he'd have the stuff from Todd Lee with him when he comes to work. Said you wanted it. Now I've told you."

"When's Jeff coming in?"

"Don't know for certain. He don't have a regular schedule since he's not a real employee, but I'd guess he'll be here around lunchtime. Free lunches are part of his pay for helping, you know," He hesitated then said, "Gotta go, pard. I'll let Jeff know I gave you the message."

"Thanks, Cal. Tell him I'll stop by this afternoon."

He didn't respond so I assumed he'd gone.

The heavy rain didn't stop until a little after noon, so I didn't get to Cal's until one o'clock. I wasn't the only person deciding to stay home today. Two men were in animated conversation at the bar and four women playing cards were the only occupants of the tables. Vern Gosdin's version of "Chiseled in Stone" was flowing from the jukebox and Cal was waving his arm to the music while he filled the beer cooler. Jeff was nowhere in sight.

Cal spotted me looking around. He pointed to the table

closest to the bandstand and as far from the group of women as possible. I took the hint and moved to the table as Cal headed to the small storage room beside the kitchen. Moments later, he arrived carrying a large paper sack, set it in front of me, and asked if I wanted anything to eat or drink. My healthy donuts breakfast had worn off, so I said a cheeseburger and a Diet Pepsi, proof I was serious about losing weight, or so I told myself.

He left the sack and headed to the kitchen. I didn't have to be a detective like Charles to deduce the sack contained Todd Lee's possessions. The men from the bar walked to the exit as Conway Twitty sang about Linda being on his mind. The women at the other occupied table appeared settled in for the afternoon.

I waited for Cal to return before opening the sack. I didn't have long to wait. The soothing aroma of my cheeseburger arrived seconds before Cal put the plate in front of me and his body in the chair facing me.

I took a bite of burger, a sip of Diet Pepsi, then asked about Jeff's whereabouts.

"Clueless. He bopped in, handed me the bag, said to give it to you, then boogied."

"What was his hurry?"

Cal shrugged. "I didn't have anything for him to do and he didn't stay for his free meal." He pointed at the card playing trio. "You can see how busy I am. Jeff acted all jumpy but didn't say why." He looked at the sack. "Ain't you curious about what's in it?"

I nodded. "Didn't want a dead man's stuff to interfere from enjoying this fantastic cheeseburger and the music."

Cal smiled like I'd given him a plaque naming Cal's as

having the best burger on Folly, then tilted his head toward the sack. "Why'd Jeff have the dead guy's stuff?"

I shared Jeff's explanation. Cal said it didn't ring true but would take my word for it.

I didn't disagree and continued with lunch. One of the women asked Cal to get her another glass of tea. He smiled, tipped his Stetson her direction, and said, "I'd be honored to get it for you." He looked my way, rolled his eyes, then headed to the bar.

I opened the sack, and the stench of sweaty clothes replaced the cheeseburger's aroma. I was glad I'd nearly finished lunch, as I cautiously removed a pair of well worn jeans, raggedy cargo shorts, two T shirts, underwear, and a mismatched pair of socks from the sack and set them as far from my plate as possible. The only other item was a small, bent notebook with most of its pages torn out. On the first remaining page, *Len S.* and *Joseph H.* were scribbled diagonally across the lined sheet. Nothing else. The next three pages were blank followed by one with *25k* crossed out. The next line had *50k* underlined three times. Nothing else was written in the book.

Cal delivered the tea to the woman then returned to my table.

"That's all that was there?"

I said it was.

"What's in the notebook?"

I showed him the two pages with writing on them.

"Who're Len and Joseph?"

I wanted to say how should I know, but limited my response to, "Don't know."

"Let's try another question. What's the deal with the numbers?"

"Don't know for certain, but Jeff thought Todd Lee was blackmailing someone. The 50k could be the amount."

"Hefty amount. Back home in Texas, that'd be enough dough to choke a porcupine. Must've had something good on somebody. Think good ole Len and Joseph had something to do with it?"

"Could be."

"Who do you think he was blackmailing?"

If I knew that, I wouldn't be here; I'd be talking with the police. Instead of stating the obvious, I said, "Don't know."

"How're you going to figure it out, pard?"

I hadn't been counting, but suspected Cal and I had exceeded a reasonable number of *don't know* or similar responses to each question in a fifteen-minute period, so I said, "I'm working on it."

I finished lunch, Cal left to check on three men who'd arrived and was leaning against the bar, I stuffed Todd's possessions in the sack, left money on the table for my food, then headed to the exit. I heard Cal yell at my back, "You'll figure it out," as George Jones began "I Always Get Lucky With You."

Would I get lucky figuring out who the killer was before he killed again?

I seriously doubted it would result in anything useful, but when I got home, I fired up the computer and Googled the two names from Todd's notebook. A quick search told me I'd have a better chance of finding the Loch Ness Monster in my bathtub than finding anything helpful on the Internet about Len S. or Joseph H., and that was combining the names with Charleston, Folly, or Savannah, the cities where both the Robinsons, the Rices, and Todd had resided or worked.

The numbers from the notebook would be even more difficult, so I didn't try. While nothing was that helpful, it reinforced my belief that Todd was trying to blackmail someone and as Cal had said, for a hefty amount. I chuckled to myself thinking all I needed to do now was connect a name to the killer.

Chapter Thirty-One

Waking without the pounding headache or rain was a plus. I'm getting too old for running around playing boy detective, okay, senior citizen non detective. Either way, it takes a toll on a body. I headed to Bert's for my usual nutritious breakfast. To my relief, no one was there to ambush me or to impart unwanted knowledge. I grabbed a cinnamon Danish, a cup of coffee, and headed home to enjoy a quiet breakfast and to do nothing. I finished breakfast and was still sipping coffee when my quiet midmorning was interrupted by the ringing phone.

"Thank the Gods you're still alive." Charles said. "Was beginning to worry." Charles's less than normal greeting crushed my hope for a telemarketer.

"Sorry, Charles, didn't know I stressed you."

"I'll let it slide."

"Thanks. What's up?" I asked, knowing it wasn't a call to check on my health and wellbeing.

"I was taking a late morning stroll and thought what

better place to go than to Loggerhead's for lunch. I was sitting on the deck looking at the humongous fake spider web covering the front of the VW bar when I decided I couldn't eat without my best bud, so instead I decided to walk next door and check out the haunted house."

I waited for the other shoe to drop, but nothing came so figured it was my turn to speak.

"That's considerate," I said, not masking the sarcasm. "Are you inviting me to lunch?"

"I'm standing in front of the house that until a few days ago was haunted. They're about finished with the renovation. I was thinking you could join me for a walk through."

He must've forgotten the luncheon invitation.

"I didn't realize we were purchasing the house and needed a walk through."

"Okay, smarty, John and Bri might be here and there're questions we need answered. Besides, aren't you curious how the house looks."

"You know curiosity killed the cat."

"That's why I'm a dog person. See you in five."

Three minutes later, I pulled in the driveway at the former haunted house to find Charles leaning on the handrail leading to the entry and looking at his wrist. His imaginary watch was apparently telling him I was late. The glories of Charles time.

"You're late and you even drove." Charles left his perch and walked over to the car.

"Sorry, my teleporter is broken."

"Cute. Let's go inside."

The only other vehicle on the haunted house's property was John and Bri's black Ford truck, or I assumed it was theirs since the company logo was on the driver's door and a large ghost sticker was on the back window promoting Lowcountry Paranormal Investigations. I suppose the workers had already finished, so why not head up the stairs to see if one or both Rices were inside?

We approached as a sour taste surfaced from the pit of my stomach. I really need a vacation from retirement.

"Hello! John, you here?" Charles booming voice echoed through the empty house.

"Hey good looking, what can I help you with?" Bri said, as she bopped around the corner and spotted Charles.

"Oh, hi Chris," she said as she saw me behind Charles. She smiled and added, "What are you all doing here?" Her blond ponytail was tied with a pink ribbon. She still reminded me of a bouncy puppy full of life and innocence. I reminded myself looks can be deceiving.

I returned her smile and said, "Guess I'm not the good looking one."

"You're funny. Who's your friend?"

"Bri, this is Charles Fowler."

"Nice to meet you, Charles."

"You, too, Bri," Charles said. "I've heard a lot about you, but your beauty surpasses anything I've been told."

Bri blushed and about that time a voice came from the hallway.

"Chris, Charles, great to see you. What brings you to our project?"

"Charles told me it was almost complete, and we wanted to see how the house looks, if that's okay."

Bri turned to her husband. "You have all sorts of secrets. You knew Charles and never thought to introduce me to such a charming man."

John laughed. "Answered your own question. I don't

need the competition." John put his arm around Bri's waist and moved her away from Charles.

Bri said, "Would you like the grand tour or prefer to explore on your own?"

"Bri, John," I said, "we don't want to take you away from your work, but a tour would be great."

Charles nodded.

John said, "We're touching up paint where electricians moved some duplex outlets. A tour will kill two birds. I can show you around while checking to see if anything else needs attention."

The four of us walked through the house with John pointing out what had been done and Bri detailed any unresolved issues. I was impressed how different the house looked from the last time I was here. It had a light, airy beach feel with high end finishes giving it a sophisticated look. There'd be no way anyone could walk through and be reminded of its recent past as a haunted house. The tour ended in the kitchen, but my eyes skipped over the marble countertop and went straight to the pantry.

"Chris," John said as he noticed me looking at the closed door, "like to see the pantry?" He chuckled. "I guarantee no dead bodies."

Charles answered for me. "Of course, we would."

John opened the door and stood to the side so we could look in. I didn't remember the pantry being so large, but then again, the last time I was in it there was a dead guy taking my focus off the rest of the room.

John and Bri remained in the kitchen where Bri said, "So gentleman, what do you think?" Her pride was evident.

Charles said, "It's great. Wouldn't mind living here myself. It'd give me a bit more wiggle room."

About a million times more, I thought, but said, "You've done a fantastic job. The Robinsons are lucky to have found you to do the project. They'll be happy here."

John frowned and shook his head. "The Robinsons will never be happy with anything or anyone. They're the most unhappy, miserable people I've had the displeasure of working with. Made me rethink my business. Perhaps I should deal only with the dead, they're better company."

Bri patted John's large hand. "What John's trying to say is thank you. It means a lot that you think the house turned out well."

"I'm sorry Chris, Charles. Thanks for the complements. We take pride in our work and it means the world when people appreciate our dedication, ideas, and work."

"I understand. From what I've experienced and heard about the Robinsons, they think they're, umm, special."

Charles laughed. "Special is Chris speak for pain in the ass."

I wasn't ready to go down that path and said, "Thanks again for the tour. We've bothered you enough. We'll let you get back to work."

Charles snapped his finger. "Chris, isn't there something you wanted to ask Bri?"

"Thanks, I almost forgot." I hoped my glare at Charles wasn't obvious.

"Bri, I saw someone outside Mike Stone's funeral on East Huron the other day and thought it might've been you."

Bri looked down before answering in a not so cheerful voice, "Yes, I was sort of there."

John glared at his wife but didn't say anything.

I said, "Did you know Mike?"

"Chris, you know John and I study the paranormal and everything involving that realm. I've always had a curiosity about witchcraft. Not the stuff you see on television or in movies but real life practices. I was in Charleston talking to Stormy at her shop and she mentioned the funeral she'd be attending on Folly. Thought it'd be a chance to observe."

"Why didn't you come in?"

"The Stones don't know me. I didn't want to disrespect anyone or impose. That's why I stayed near the street. I was able to see some of the ritual. I left as quickly as I could hoping not to be seen. The last thing the family needed was some uninvited outsider showing up. Figured it'd be my only time to see what a Wiccan funeral was like. Thought you saw me but didn't want to stick around to be sure. Did anyone else see me?"

"Not that I know of, why?"

"I've felt bad ever since then. It was a sacred time and there I was watching out of mere curiosity. If the family had seen me it would've been awful."

John wrapped his arm around her shoulder and said,"Bri would never want to hurt or interfere with anyone." He smiled. "Occasionally her curiosity overtakes common sense."

"No harm done, Bri," I said. "Charles and I really need to get going and let you two finish before the good doctor has a cow about the house."

"He has no reason to. They'll be moving in right after Halloween like he was promised," John said, as he walked us to the door leaving Bri in the kitchen.

As we waved bye to John, Charles said, "Can you give me a ride home? Weather looks like it's going to turn nasty."

As I figured, Charles's Loggerhead's luncheon plan was a ruse to get us invited into the house.

On the way to his apartment, he said, "Do you believe Bri's story about why she was at Mike's funeral?"

"It makes sense considering her interest in the occult and not wanting to intrude on the ceremony."

"Yes, sounds like a perfect excuse to be there but it also sounds like a perfect excuse to be there if you know what I mean." Charles eyes drilled a hole into the side of my head. "You know killers often attend the funeral of guys or gals they've killed."

They do on television shows and in novels, the extent of Charles's investigative training. Instead of pointing that out, I said, "You're right. If she thought I saw her, she had time to come up with a reason for being there."

Rain started pounding the windshield and put a damper on our conversation, I suspected Charles was thinking the same thing I was. Was Bri an innocent woman with unique interests or a killer with the ability to come up with a decent excuse?

Chapter Thirty-Two

If Bri was telling the truth about why she was snooping around the funeral, there was a good chance she wasn't the killer, nor would her husband have a motive, at least not an obvious one. That brought me back to square one, or somewhere near that proverbial starting place. Then I remembered Charles saying Dude had talked with Todd Lee, but that was about all he'd said. Why not visit the surf shop to see if Dude remembered more than he'd shared with Charles? Even if he hadn't, the rain had stopped, and a walk would do me good.

The surf shop with no capital letters in the name was on Center Street near its intersection with Ashley Avenue. The single story, wood frame, elevated structure with an exterior displaying many surfboard sized decals promoting surfing equipment was as much a staple on Folly's main drag as was Planet Follywood, the Crab Shack, and the Sand Dollar private club.

I was greeted at the door, using the term greeted loosely,

by Stephon, one of Dude's employees who would be the winner hands down if the island ever had a rudest employee competition.

"What?" he said with a smirk after he couldn't ignore me since I was a foot in front of him.

"Dude here?"

Stephon's smirk intensified as he pointed his arm covered with more tattoos than Dennis Rodman has on his entire body toward the back of the store. It was his way of "politely" indicating the store's owner was in his office.

"Thanks, Stephon," I said faking a smile.

He muttered either, "You're welcome," or a profanity before turning back to his more important task of thumbing through an issue of *SURFER* magazine.

Dude's office door was closed so I shook off my rude welcome from Stephon and knocked.

"What?" Dude yelled.

I opened the door, stuck my head in, and said, "Dude, have a few minutes?"

Dude was in his late sixties, looked like a cross between Arlo Guthrie and Willie Nelson, and wore one of his many tie dye shirts featuring a large peace symbol on the front.

"Whoops. My bad, Chrisster. Thought be tatted peep Rudester knockin'." He waved me in.

I'm often wary meeting with Dude without Charles, someone who could translate much of what Dude was saying, although Rudester could only be Stephon.

"Got a question," I said, reducing my words to match the man who never grasped using ten words when two would sort of do.

Dude smiled as he pointed to the chair in front of his cluttered desk. I moved the stack of shirts, sat, and waited to see if he had anything else to say before I asked the question. He didn't, so I said, "Dude, you were telling Charles a few days ago that Todd Lee applied for a job."

He nodded. "Be sitting right here. Pluto be eatin' food beside desk."

I waited for more, but apparently Dude had exceeded his word quota. Pluto was his Australian Terrier that looked like a miniature version of its master.

"Charles said you didn't have anything available."

"Chrisster, this be month ten. Business sucky. Rudester handles peeps surfin' in. No be needin' overstaffing."

Fortunately, I understood all that.

"Did he fill out an application?"

Dude leaned forward. "You be moonlightin' as EEOC cop?"

I smiled. "No, trying to learn more about him."

"In dark ages, had job wanting peeps fill application. Called it doin' Dude diligence." He chuckled then tapped his head with his forefinger. "Waste of time. Job wanting peeps only gave employers who say boss things about them. Past bosses also lied about how good past peeps did jobs. Waste of time." He held his arms out. I assumed indicating how big a waste of time. "Most peeps I hire spent most of life on wrong side of law. Need new chance."

Rudester Stephon came to mind. "I understand. Do you remember anything Todd Lee said that may help me figure out why he was killed?"

"He be all jittery. Can you believe, he afearin' *moi*?"

Yes, I thought, but didn't say it. "Maybe he got nervous about job interviews. That's not uncommon."

Dude nodded. "Pluto jumped in his lap, got him relax-in'. Told me last job he got payroll check was in Savannah, G. A."

"A surf shop?"

He shook his head. "Medical office, but he not be doc."

"What'd he do there?"

"Highlight be getting fired."

"Dude, what was his job before he was terminated?"

He shrugged. "He not bigwig."

I figured that was all I'd get from Dude about Todd's job duties.

"Do you recall the name of the office where he worked?"

"Didn't ask. Not surf shop, so didn't care."

"Do you remember anything else he said?"

Dude smiled, nodded his head, and said, "Be stoked about knowing Pluto."

"I don't blame him. Pluto's a great dog."

Dude's smile covered his entire face, then he pointed to me. "My turn for questions?"

"What might they be?"

"Might be how many peeps live in Tangier, but not. Question one, you know first name of candy corn be chicken food? First box had rooster on front. Believe that?"

"Huh?"

"Halloween candy."

"Oh," I said, like he'd made perfectly good sense. "You learn that from Charles?"

"Nope, television. Be Halloween Eve, Eve. Thought you needed Halloween factoid."

"Thanks."

"Question two, you going to catch slimeball that wiped

out Todd and my new, and now dead, friend Mike the witch?"

"Trying to."

"Cool."

Dude asked if I wanted to leave out the back door to avoid Stephon, or that's what I think he meant.

I said, "Cool."

Chapter Thirty-Three

On the walk home, I reviewed what Dude had shared about Todd Lee. All I'd learned was that Todd had worked in a medical office in Savannah, Dude no longer checked references, and chicken feed was the original name of candy corn. By the time I reached my yard, I decided there was no reason to be stressing over it by myself. I could get with Charles and between the two of us come up with, umm, come up with something. My kitchen cabinet was as bare as Old Mother Hubbard's Cupboard, so instead of going in the house, I stopped at Bert's for snacks, or as Charles would say, brain food. I left the store with more junk food than needed for a teenage girl's slumber party before calling Charles to invite him over.

"What's wrong? Who died?" Charles said instead of a simple *hello*. My dislike of Caller ID deepened.

"Nothing's wrong. As far as I know, no one died. Want to come over and try to figure out where we are with, umm, the murders?"

"About time you admitted that's what we need to do."

I imagined Charles patting himself on the back for convincing me it was what we needed to do.

"You coming?"

"On my way. Have anything resembling food or should I give you time to go shopping before I show up?"

"I have plenty." The phone went dead. If nothing else, Charles doesn't disappoint.

I put the chips in a bowl on the kitchen table and added a package of Oreos on the table beside the chips, poured Charles a Coke and myself a Diet Coke when I heard the front door open and a cane tapping on the floor heading my way.

Charles removed his Tilley and leaned his cane against the counter before staring at the table. "Wow, buttering me up for something. You have the name of the killer or killers to go with this feast?"

I smiled at his definition of feast, and said, "I talked with Dude. Wanted to see if he knew more about Todd Lee. I remembered you said he'd interviewed Todd for a job, but that was all. As you know, it's hard to get everything from listening to Dude's stories."

"Where did you see Dude?"

"His shop."

"Went on your own, no translator, no me?"

"I understood most of what he said."

"By understanding Dudespeak, you might've attained local status."

"I've lived here more than a decade."

"Yeah, but you weren't born here." Charles tapped his fingers on the table like he'd made a profound statement.

"You weren't either. For that matter, most people I know here weren't."

He sighed, grabbed an Oreo, and stared at me.

Not hearing a comeback, I said, "Charles, you ready to hear why I called?"

"What did you learn from Dude?"

"Todd's last job before coming here was at a medical office in Savannah."

"Which one? What did he do there?"

"Dude didn't know which one or what kind of medical office."

"Hmm, interesting, worthless, but interesting," Charles said as he reached for another Oreo.

"I have more," I said, knowing I was in for grief for not telling him sooner. "Todd had a notebook with two first names in it along with what appears to be a dollar amount."

Charles waved a hand in my face, "You—"

"I'm not finished."

He shook his head, moved his hand away from my face, and said, "Well, what are you waiting for?"

"Jeff Hildebrand left Todd Lee's possessions with Cal who gave them to me. And, before you ask, I googled the two names but came up dry."

Charles glared at me. "You just have the dead man's notebook and didn't think to share that monster clue with the only person who could help you find the killer." He grabbed another Oreo and shoved it to his mouth.

"Charles, I just got the things from Cal." Okay, *just got* was a bit of a stretch, but I wasn't in the mood to be lectured.

"In the spirit of catching a killer, I'll let that oversight, gross oversight go."

"You're too kind," I said, oozing sarcasm.

"So, we think Todd was blackmailing someone before he came to Folly. According to Dude in a meeting I wasn't invited to, Todd worked in a medical office in Savannah. There's a notebook that was left for you at Cal's that you got when you went there without inviting me, a notebook with a dollar amount and first names of guys he may've been blackmailing someone about. That cover it?"

"Wordy but sums it up. What are reasons for blackmailing someone?"

Charles rubbed his chin, looked at the ceiling, then said, "Sex, drugs, rock and roll, murder, lies, embezzlement, deep dark secrets."

"We can take rock and roll off the list, the others, possible."

Charles smiled. "See, we've already narrowed it down. What kind of medical office?"

"I already told you I don't know, and there are probably hundreds in Savannah."

Charles nodded toward my office. "We better start looking."

I knew a computer search was futile, but so was arguing with my friend. We grabbed our drinks, the bag of Oreos, and moved to my computer.

I Googled medical offices in Savannah, Georgia, and to no surprise found numerous listed.

"Okay, Mr. Detective," I said as I looked over my shoulder at Charles, "how do you want to narrow this down?"

"You're the Google finder guy. What do you suggest?"

"I could Google medical offices with best blackmail opportunities?"

Charles stared at me. "So, you have no idea?"

"Yep."

"Then why are we looking at the computer?"

"It was your idea."

"You're thinking it wasn't one of my best."

"Yep," I repeated. "If Todd learned something where he worked, it could be about a patient, someone working in the office, someone who visited the office, someone who cleaned the office, on and on. And, it may not have had anything to do with where he worked."

"Chris, you sure know how to fog up a mirror."

"Yep."

Charles snapped his fingers. "Whoa, why didn't I think of it earlier? Who do we know who worked in a medical office in Savannah, someone who just happens to own the very house where Todd Lee took his last breath?"

I wondered when Charles was going to figure that out. I didn't want to start with that fact since Charles would've proclaimed that solved the case closing out other possibilities. I also didn't remind him he'd already said Fred or his wife was the killer just the other day. I said, "Dr. Fred Robinson."

"There you go. We figured out who killed Todd Lee and I suppose Mike Stone. You better call Chief LaMond, or Detective Adair, or the Charleston newspaper, TV and radio stations and let them know." He pointed to my phone before stuffing another Oreo in his mouth.

My strategy of not mentioning Dr. Robinson's *medical office* in Savannah had failed "And tell them what? Fred Robinson worked in a dental office in Savannah, so he has to be the killer?"

"No, tell them he's the killer because Todd was blackmailing him because of the names in the notebook and for the amount that was in there. Duh."

"Charles, I must've missed it. What proof do we have? Why was he blackmailing the good dentist?"

"Chris, we can't do everything. Don't you think it's time the police did some of the work?"

"Charles."

He interrupted, "Hold it, you said you Googled the two names from the notebook?"

"Yes," I said, omitting the word halfheartedly since all I had was first names and what I assumed to be a last initial.

"Sure there was nothing?"

"Yep."

Charles shook his head. "So, all those chips and Oreos and we came up with nothing except Dr. Robinson is the killer, but we have no way to prove it."

"Yep."

Chapter Thirty-Four

Never having had children to take trick or treating or willingly attending Halloween parties as an adult because I hated the idea of dressing up like someone I'm not, the October holiday was never high on my list of favorite holidays. With Halloween only hours rather than days away, this one topped all the others I've experienced in both horror and nightmares—topped them by far.

My talk with Charles yesterday only uncovered more questions. Was Dr. Robinson the killer? Should I call Chief LaMond to let her know what we suspected? The logical side of my brain overruled the Hardy Boys side. We had no proof, just a bunch of disjointed facts and the coincidence that Todd Lee and Dr. Robinson had lived in Savannah. I was still going over the possibilities when the phone rang.

Before the caller could say anything, I started the conversation with a brilliant and seldom used greeting on Folly, "Hello."

"We're in luck," Charles said, his voice a couple of

octaves higher than normal. "I just saw a big ole moving truck at the haunted house. Two guys the size of bull elephants were unloading tables, boxes, and a bunch of filing cabinets."

"Who is this?" I said, hoping to tamper his excitement.

"Funny. Ready to do some grade A snooping?"

"See if I have this right. You're out casing the former haunted house. You see a moving truck and decide to call your friend for some breaking and entering? How'd I do?"

"About sums it up."

"Charles, with all due respect, have you lost your mind? Why would I agree?"

"If Todd was blackmailing Fred about something that happened in the office, I figure the chances are good some information would be in those filing cabinets at his house and not in his office where someone could find it. That's where I'd keep my secrets."

"Did you ever own a filing cabinet?"

Today was let's send Charles over the edge day, primarily to deflect what he wanted to do.

He sighed, then said, "Not the point. You coming?"

"Charles, it's the middle of the morning. What makes you think the house will be empty? What about the movers? Or, what about John and Bri, or, umm, how about the Robinsons, you know, the owners?"

"Well, Mr. Know It All, it's the perfect time. The moving van pulled out ten minutes ago. The only other vehicle here was Erica Robinson's. She drove off when the moving van left."

"Charles, what—"

"Whoa, there's more. Best of all, the fog's so thick nobody would see us going in. Okay, your turn."

"What about Fred Robinson? He could be in the house, and you didn't see him. It's not like you have an infrared camera checking for occupants?"

I knew this was a losing battle. I needed to go to keep Charles from getting himself in more trouble, but that didn't mean I had to give in quickly.

"Infrared cameras. What a great idea for our detective agency. Why didn't you ever suggest that before?"

Out of all the reasons I gave for not breaking into someone's house, Charles focused on infrared cameras.

"Because we are not detectives. This is a bad idea."

"Oh, ye of little faith, it's the perfect idea and time. I called the dental office and according to Mildred, a helpful lady who answered the phone, Dr. Robinson is scheduled to be there all day. Said she was sorry about my aching tooth, but he didn't have a free appointment until late next week."

I'd be wasting words trying to stop him.

"I'll be there in a few minutes. Don't do anything until I get there." I omitted the word *stupid* after *anything* and hung up.

Fortunately, the short drive to the last haunted house I will ever enter was quick. If it'd taken longer, I would've talked myself out of the absurdity of breaking into the private residence of a person who might or might not be a killer. Then again, this entire month has been nothing but one absurdity after another, starting with Charles wanting to relive a childhood memory of attending a haunted house. Now he's on the verge of breaking in a house to live out his adult fantasy of being a detective. Truth be known, I blame him for all this, but a big part of me wants answers as much as he does.

I parked and spotted Charles leaning against the garage

in the former haunted house's back yard. He was wearing his long sleeve, black sweatshirt with NYPD in white on the chest.

He smiled and said, "Ready to get the party started?"

"What're the chances of talking you out of this crazy idea?"

"Chris, have I ever led you astray?"

"You really want me to answer that?"

"Umm, no. You know you want answers as much as I do. This is our chance before the Robinsons move in."

It was hard to argue with him since I did want to know. Besides, all we had for the police was a hunch, and that was based on Dude saying Todd Lee worked at a medical office in Savannah and that he may've been trying to blackmail Fred Robinson because, umm, because why?

"Charles, I'm trying to stop you from doing anything stupid, well more stupid than breaking into a house that's not yours."

"The house is nobody's yet. John and Bri have finished work on it and the Robinsons haven't moved in, so it's abandoned. It's fair game." Charles had already headed to the back stairs like that said it all.

I hoped he was right.

Chapter Thirty-Five

Charles's less than brilliant idea began to sink in as we approached the house. More accurately, I think we were approaching the house, but I wasn't sure since a dense sea fog enveloped the structure making it nearly indistinguishable from the gray fog.

"Good news, Chris. There's not a chance anyone will see us break in," said my glass is half full friend.

"Good news, right."

"Looks more like a haunted house now than it did when we stumbled on Todd Lee, doesn't it?"

I didn't know about that but was certain my nerves were frayed as we reached the back stairs. I nearly missed the first step when the sound of a vehicle speeding past the house startled me. I was about ready to turn and hightail it home but reminded myself while this ill conceived adventure could turn out bad, it couldn't possibly be as bad as if Charles did it alone. Or could it?

"Keep a watch for anyone coming," Charles said as he bent to see how to get in the back door.

"The fog's so thick I wouldn't see anyone until they were up here with us."

Charles didn't own credit cards, so he was slipping a small putty knife between the door and the frame to push the latch bolt enough to unlock it. I was impressed he thought to bring the tool, but this wasn't a good time to praise his ability to commit a crime.

Another vehicle zipped by, but it didn't startle me nearly as much as the Halloween horror movie squeak the door made as it swung inward after Charles's successful break in.

"See, it's an omen," he said, "it wanted us to come in."

Charles's logic at its best.

It was light outside, but I had difficulty seeing more than a few feet in front of me. I was still looking around, clearly not moving fast enough for Charles, who'd already gone to the pantry, aka the room where we found Todd Lee. He turned on the overhead light and stared at five stacks of moving boxes covering half the floor.

He said, "Think there's a clue in there?"

I didn't think that deserved a response which was fortunate since he'd already started looking for ways to open the top box in the closest stack without disturbing the tape holding it shut. Instead of watching my friend, I kept looking at the spot on the floor where we'd seen Todd. I shuttered thinking of that night.

Charles had managed to loosen the tape without tearing it or the box when I thought I heard the back door squeak. Was I imagining it, was it a ghost, or was someone there?

Then I heard the back door shut. I never thought I'd prefer to see a ghost more than what I saw. Erika Robinson was standing in the doorway to the pantry. What was more frightening was the black handgun she pointed at me.

Charles was focused on the boxes and didn't see the latest addition to the pantry until Erika said, "Couldn't leave it alone, could you?"

Charles pivoted so quickly that I thought Erika was going to shoot him as she twisted in his direction. His hands flew over his head.

Erika smirked and said, "Wise man." She pointed the gun at the floor. "Sit."

I had no doubt she wasn't going to let us leave the house alive, but with the boxes and filing cabinets covering much of the floor and Erika blocking the exit, I couldn't see a way out. If I could keep her talking, there was a possibility she'd make a mistake—a remote possibility, but our only hope.

I lowered myself to the floor and said, "Erika, what happened?"

She started to speak but was distracted by another vehicle passing the house. Unfortunately, she wasn't distracted enough for me to attack.

She turned back to me. "My idiot husband wasn't satisfied being a dentist. We have a good income. He was made partner in an extraordinarily successful dental practice where he could reap the rewards from several offices. That wasn't enough."

Her hand trembled as she appeared to get angrier. Perhaps getting her talking was a mistake, but I couldn't see another way to buy time.

"What do you mean?"

"He figured out he could make more, a lot more, selling oxycodone prescriptions to patients than working on their teeth." She shook her head. "Told him he was an idiot, but no, oh no, he knew better. Know what happened?"

I suspected I did but didn't see any advantage in sharing. It was her story, hopefully a long one, long enough to figure a way out of this mess.

Charles said, "What happened?"

She slowly pointed the gun at my friend. "Two deaths, that's what. Wouldn't you think someone with medical training would've known prescribing oxy to addicts might not turn out well?"

Charles said, "Len and Joseph?"

She sighed. "Knew you busybodies couldn't leave it alone. Where'd you hear about those guys?"

Erika wasn't going to leave loose ends, so if I told her we got Todd's possessions from Jeff Hildebrand I'd be signing his death warrant. "Couple of guys talking in a bar. Don't know who they were."

She uttered a profanity then said, "Fred's going to be the death of me yet."

I didn't see that happening anytime soon, but still needed her to keep talking.

"Why kill Todd Lee?"

She smiled but it appeared more of a smirk. "Who said I did?"

Charles said, "Did you?"

"Know what my idiot husband did after the oxy deaths?"

I didn't detect a confession in there but had no doubt she or her *idiot husband* had killed Todd.

"What?" Charles asked.

"He had one of his office workers shred eight patient files. Told the guy they were old and no longer patients. Fred told me he had the person shred eight files so he wouldn't get suspicious about two of them dying. Idiot."

"Todd Lee?"

She nodded. "Told me Lee was so stupid he'd never put two and two together. Know what Fred did then?"

Charles said, "What?"

"Fired Lee. How stupid is that?"

Figured it was a rhetorical question, so I remained quiet.

"Fred was partially right, I guess. Lee didn't say or do anything about it until we moved to Charleston. How were we to know Lee was here? We ran into him in Bert's one day when we were checking on the house. Quite a shock it was. He called Fred the next day."

Charles said, "Blackmail?"

She shook her head. "Fifty thousand dollars and Fred would never hear from him again. The cash would erase it from his head, so he claimed." She continued shaking her head. "Never hear from him again, he said. Never until he wanted more. How stupid did he think we were? I couldn't have that, could I?" The sound of another vehicle broke Erika's rant. She looked toward the street but didn't let it distract from her outburst. "Know what Fred said?"

I didn't so I remained quiet.

Silence was outside Charles's comfort zone. "What?"

I thought I heard the back door squeak, but after a few seconds realized it was wishful thinking. Where was Chucky or Blackbeard when we needed them?

"Fred said fifty K was more than Todd had ever seen in his life and would be thrilled having it."

I said, "You didn't agree?"

"Not for a second. I told Fred I'd deliver the money, so he would be at work in case anything bad happened.

Good alibi, you know. He thought that was a great idea. Idiot."

I said, "You had no intention of paying him?"

"No way."

Charles said, "What happened?"

"Called and told Todd we'd meet him here. The haunted house crew wasn't here in the morning and the contractors were only working two days a week until the haunted house was over. Come to think of it, that was supposed to be tomorrow. Could hear Todd jumping with excitement over the phone." She gave a sinister laugh that would have been perfect in any haunted house. "He came in like he owned the world. Wasn't how he left, was it?"

"Why an ice pick instead of that?" I said as I nodded toward the gun.

"Good question. You're smarter than the man I married. I knew what I was going to do when I got here, but Fred didn't since he thought I was handing the blackmailer a stack of cash." She chuckled. "When he got home from his office, umm, his alibi, I said Lee tried to attack me, wanted to take the fifty thousand and anything else I had in my purse, and no telling what else he wanted to do to me. So, I grabbed the nearest weapon I could find. Said the ice pick was in the kitchen." She chuckled. "Sort of forgot to mention I brought it with me. You see, I had no choice but to stab him."

Charles said, "He believed that?"

"Told you he was an idiot. Yeah, took more than a few tears, but he finally agreed I didn't have a choice. So sad for poor Todd. Know what Fred wanted to do?"

I guessed, "Go to the police?"

"Can you believe that? Well, that wasn't going to happen. Took more tears to get him to agree."

I said, "Why kill Mike Stone?"

"Didn't want to, but Todd told me before he met the ice pick that he'd talked to an attorney. He figured that'd give him leverage. Anyway, I was afraid he told the lawyer about the oxy overdoses."

Charles said, "Did he?"

"Don't know but couldn't take a chance. Took me the longest time to figure out who the attorney was. Todd only referred to him as Mike. Know how many lawyers there are in Charleston named Mike or Michael? If I didn't hear him talking, arguing, with a kid at the grocery, I'd still be looking for him." She looked at the weapon in her hand, at Charles, then at me. "Guess it's time for this little gathering to come to an end. It's been—"

A sound came from the doorway. It wasn't Chucky, Blackbeard, or the police coming to the rescue.

Lugh nearly filled the entire opening. Desmond stood behind him and shouted, "*Greim*!"

The word was barely out of his mouth when Lugh bounded into the room and with his massive jaws grabbed Erika's outstretched arm holding the gun.

I reached the gun before she pulled the trigger. Lugh still gripped Erika's arm. Desmond stood back and watched like it was something he saw every day. He then gave a command I couldn't understand. Lugh let go of her arm, took a step back, and sat.

I looked around to find something to secure Erika and noticed Lugh's oversized leash. I asked Desmond if I could use it to tie Erika. He smiled, one of the few times I'd seen that emotion on his face, as he unhooked the leash and handed it to me. Erika wasn't going to be restrained easily. She twisted and tried to bite Charles's hand as he maneuvered her around so I could get to both hands. Lugh was no more than three feet away from her yet remained still. Erika noticed the dog's eyes following her every move. She wisely stopped resisting enough for me to tighten the leash around her wrists.

After she was secure, it took another thirty seconds before I caught my breath enough to dial 911. Charles held onto the leash making sure Erika couldn't loosen the restraint. Desmond moved closer and put his arm around Lugh's neck.

I went to the front room to open the door for the police, stared at the street, and swore I would never attend another haunted house no matter how much anyone begged. Period.

Chapter Thirty-Six

Over the years, I've attended numerous Christmas parades on Folly and had never heard as many sirens as I heard approaching a former haunted house on Halloween Eve. At least three, possibly more, patrol cars were rushing to our location, plus the distinct sound of two fire engines. Fewer than three minutes after my 911 call, the drive, much of the side yard and along West Arctic Avenue in front of the house were filling with emergency vehicles.

Officer Trula Bishop was first up the stairs, asked if I was okay, receiving my assurance that not only I was, but so were the other three people in the house. She either exhaled from excitement knowing I was okay or was trying to catch her breath from jogging up the steps.

Either way, she gave me a police officer's stare and said, "Chris, what pile of manure have you stepped in this time? The last time I was here, you were standing over a dead body."

"Trula, if you'll follow me, I'll take you to the person

who stabbed the man whose body I'd been standing over and the person who killed Mike Stone."

Before I could lead her through the house to the pantry, Officer Spencer rushed up the steps, with a hand resting on his holstered firearm. He didn't say it, but from the look on his face, he shared Officer Bishop's sentiments about me. Instead of explaining what'd happened, I led both officers to the pantry filled with filing cabinets, moving boxes, Erika, Charles, Desmond, and Lugh who was occupying the most space. Both officers saw the Irish Wolfhound and stepped back. I suggested that Desmond escort Lugh to the back porch until the officers removed Erika. Bishop said it was an excellent idea.

After the room was one sixteen-year-old and one massive canine lighter, Bishop asked what was going on. Charles and I tag teamed her with the explanation while Spencer told the EMTs who'd entered the house that their services wouldn't be needed. He then helped Erika to her feet and out the door while the rest of us moved to the large front room.

Chief LaMond was next to arrive. She watched Spencer escort Erika to his patrol vehicle then silently listened to Bishop's explanation of what'd happened, shook her head a few times when Bishop told her why Charles and I were here, then asked Bishop to take notes while Charles and I explained everything a second time.

Thirty minutes later, which, I might add, seemed like three hours, the Chief and Officer Bishop appeared satisfied with our explanations and asked us to come to her office the next day to review and verify the events as recorded by Bishop. She added that Detective Adair would be contacting us later today or tomorrow.

I lied and said, "I look forward to it."

Cindy smiled and finally got around to asking if Charles and I were okay.

Charles said, "Fine as frog's hair on Halloween."

Cindy gave him a skeptical look, one he often receives, and said, "Don't suppose a President said that?"

She didn't wait for an answer before turning to me. "You okay?"

This time I was truthful. "I will be."

Two more officers arrived and were dismissed by the Chief. She then said. "Chris, I'll give you and Charles a few more minutes in here to, umm, catch your breath. Can I trust you to lock up on the way out?"

"Of course, Chief," Charles said.

Cindy shook her head one more time before heading to the door.

Desmond and Lugh were still waiting on the back deck. Desmond held his arms around his black Sisters of Mercy T shirt to stay warm. The temperature must've dropped ten degrees since we'd entered the house. I asked if he wanted to come inside where it was warmer. He nodded and led Lugh back in. Lugh stared at the door to the pantry and Desmond who'd watched the recent activity in the house through the back door window assured his canine pal the bad woman was gone. I didn't know how much English Lugh knew, but he moved close to Desmond and sat.

"Desmond, what were you doing here?" Charles asked the question that was also on my mind.

He lowered his head and barely above a whisper said, "You won't tell Mom, will you?"

I couldn't make that promise considering what'd happened. "Not unless I have to."

"I came around the haunted house most nights it was open. Stood across the street or out there." He nodded toward the back yard. "Mom didn't want me to be here, said if people saw me, they'd start associating our religion with bad things haunted houses make popular, or something like that."

Charles said, "Like knife flailing serial killers and pirates?"

"Sort of. Anyway, I'm interested in the occult, mysticism, conjuring, stuff like that."

Charles said, "Because of your religion?"

Charles, let the young man finish, I thought.

"Sort of. I'm also interested in finding out more about Christianity." He smiled. "Even attended one of Preacher Burl's services. Roisin wondered why. I told her not to worry. I wasn't

converting. Told her I was scouting the competition."

A sense of humor from Desmond. What other surprises did he hold?

"Desmond," I said, "why were you here today?"

"Mr. Landrum, even when the haunted house wasn't open, I liked hanging around. I've watched the construction guys from back there." He again nodded toward the back yard. "Lugh liked it, too. I don't much, but he likes people. Likes to watch them. Strange, I know. Anyway, days before the guy was killed in there, I saw a woman going in a few times. Thought she must've been part of the bunch working on the house, but whenever she was there, the workers weren't around."

Charles said, "Did you recognize her?"

"Not until today. Lugh and I were back there. Saw you two, umm, break in, then she went up the steps. I didn't know what was going on. Thought she was meeting you, so Lugh and I sneaked up the steps. We weren't breaking in. Honest. The door wasn't closed, so I sort of pushed it all the way open. That's when we heard you talking in that storage room or whatever it's called."

"Pantry," Charles the trivia king interrupted.

"Yeah, pantry. Anyway, I heard her tell you about … about killing Dad." He wiped a tear from his cheek before continuing. "She had that gun and I figured if she killed that other guy and dad, she was going to shoot you two. That's when I told Lugh to attack." He reached down and patted Lugh's head.

I wanted to put my arm around the young man but was afraid Lugh might not take too kindly to it. Instead, I said, "Desmond, we're glad you did. You saved our lives."

He gave a weak smile. "Guess so. Something good came from me snooping around the haunted house all those times. Maybe Mom will be proud of me."

"Desmond, she will be."

He grinned. "Suppose I'd better get home. I don't know what needs to be done, but Mom said there were some things we needed to do to prepare for spreading Dad's ashes tomorrow. Halloween's a special day for us, you know."

I said, "Desmond, before you go, let me ask you something. Did you say the back door wasn't closed when you got here?"

"It was open, Mr. Landrum."

I smiled. "Thanks again for saving us."

Charles added, "You too, Lugh."

I didn't know exactly what would happen tomorrow, but there was no doubt Desmond and Lugh saved two lives on Halloween Eve.

Chapter Thirty-Seven

Halloween had finally arrived. I was more excited than I had ever been for the holiday to get here. It wasn't because of the normal Halloween festivities, but because I was alive. To many, the holiday was a celebration of death. I was celebrating life.

After two cups of coffee, I decided the best way to celebrate was to have a gathering of friends, old and maybe some new, to remind all of us the importance of living each day as if it's our last. I smiled thinking how absurd it was to start planning a Halloween party on Halloween morning. Then again, the absurd is often normal on Folly. Besides, I'm not big on costume parties or decorating for the holiday, so why not? After all, the most important part of any party was having guests you enjoyed being with.

I couldn't afford to waste time but needed to make a call before going shopping. If I didn't call Charles, I'd never hear the end of it, plus, he can spread the word quicker than any method of communication known to man.

He answered on the second ring with, "Happy Halloween! Been held at gunpoint lately?"

Ignoring his comment, I said, "Was thinking of having a get together later today."

He responded with a loud sigh and, "Nothing like waiting until the last minute to invite me. Thought we were friends."

"You're the first person I've invited. Thought it'd be nice having a small gathering with friends to try to get our lives back to normal."

"I don't do normal very good, but it's not a bad idea. Who's on the list and what can I do?"

"Invite anyone you think would like to come. Before you ask, no, not the entire island, only our friends. Charles, this isn't a big event. One more thing, no costumes."

"No costumes? So, you're not going to the costume contest at the community center?"

"Charles!"

"Okay, okay, sounds like someone doesn't have the Halloween spirit."

"That's right."

Another sigh, followed by, "What time is the no costume Halloween event going to start? I'd vote for four, so it doesn't conflict with the Witches Dance at the County Park."

"Wouldn't want you to miss that event, so four is fine. Remember, no costumes and not the entire island."

"On it."

I made a list of items needed and since I had nothing in the house fit to serve guests, a trip to Harris Teeter was mandatory. On the way, I stopped at Barb's Books to invite its lovely owner to the event. I hoped she hadn't heard about yesterday's traumatic events. She wouldn't be happy regardless, but the blow would be softened if she heard it from me, or so I hoped.

"I was beginning to think you'd vanished in all of this fog of late," she said as I entered the bookstore.

"Vanished, not really. Been busy."

"Retirement must be exhausting," she said with a smile. "Want some coffee?"

"No thanks. I'm on the way to Harris Teeter, which brings me to the reason I stopped by."

"You don't have to get me anything. I can shop for myself, but thanks for the offer."

"Good to know. Next time you can do my grocery shopping. I'm having an impromptu Halloween party this afternoon around four and wanted to personally invite you."

"Then it's after you enter the costume contest at the community center?"

"Have you been talking to Charles?"

"No, why?"

"Never mind."

She smiled. "Well, I have to rearrange my busy schedule and close early, but I can squeeze you in. What do I need to bring?"

"Just yourself. One more thing, it's not a costume party."

"Darn, I was going to wear my sexy zombie outfit." She laughed, grabbed my arm, and gave me a kiss on the cheek.

"My loss."

Now to broach what happened yesterday. I was pleased when all she said after my abbreviated version of the traumatic event was she was glad we caught the killer. This time, she gave me a kiss on the lips. I'd dodged a possible lecture about getting involved. Perhaps, Halloween wasn't so bad after all.

I left the store and noticed the door to First Light open. If Preacher Burl was there, it'd save a phone call.

"Preacher, you here?" I said as I entered the foul weather sanctuary.

"Brother Chris, come in. I was getting a pot of coffee going. Want some?"

"No thanks. I'm having some friends over this afternoon and wondered if you could stop by. I know it's short notice."

"Love to, it'd be nice to get out and socialize."

"My house around four."

"Sounds good. Would you mind if I brought some people?"

"People?"

"Not sure if you know, but today Shannon and the kids will be spreading Brother Mike's ashes. I was thinking it might be nice if they had something to distract them."

"I remembered that's what they were doing. Speaking of the Stones, have you heard what happened yesterday?"

"Guess not."

I gave a shortened version of the happenings in the haunted house.

"Oh, my word. I must contact them immediately."

I told him it was a good idea and if they were up to it, they were welcome at my party.

An hour later, although it seemed like an eternity slogging up each aisle in the grocery and buying enough food and drinks to feed a small army, I arrived home. Whose idea was this party?

Time flew as I straightened the house and put out candy. I couldn't have a Halloween party without candy. I chuckled as I filled two bowls with candy corn thinking about Dude saying it'd originally been called chicken food. I also wondered if that was true. I'll take his word since I didn't have the energy or interest to Google it.

Barb was the first to arrive which surprised me since Charles is always first to anything.

"Surprised you're here early. You beat Charles."

"That was my plan," she said as she slipped past me and took a grocery bag to the kitchen counter. "I figured this was the first party you've had at your house, so you'd need a woman's touch." She then waved for me to follow her to the door.

On the way to her car, she said, "I thought you'd need help getting ready and I brought a few things you can help with."

Her passenger seat was stacked with trays of fruits, cold cuts, and cookies. If Charles did invite the entire population of the island, we'd have enough food.

As we lugged the containers in, Barb said, "Men and spur of the moment party planning never end well."

I didn't disagree.

We were in the kitchen arranging the platters when I heard the familiar sound of a cane tapping on my front door. Charles was not alone.

He said, "Finally, was thinking we were going to be left on the porch. Chris, I believe you know Cal, Dude and, of course, Pluto." Charles gestured behind him.

"I believe we've met."

If anyone had been watching, they would've thought I was having a costume party. Dude was wearing a tie dyed, long sleeve, multicolored T shirt with a giant glow in the dark peace symbol on the front. Cal had on his ageless Stetson, his rhinestone trimmed coat, and carrying his guitar case, and even Dude's dog Pluto was adorned with a rhinestone covered leash with a white cloth wrapped around his body. Charles was the most muted person on the porch wearing an orange, long sleeve University of Tennessee sweatshirt. All reminders that normal is a foreign concept on my adopted island.

Cal tipped his Stetson. "I couldn't turn down Charles's invite. Always wanted to sing "Monster Mash" at a real Halloween party. Hard to believe, but when I do it at the bar, some people laugh. Can you believe that?"

Yes, but I didn't say it.

Dude and Pluto followed Cal into the house. "Pluto plus me be chillin' when Chucky said there be a party. Here we be."

I put my arm around Charles's shoulder and whispered, "Only two and a pup. I'm shocked."

"Two more will be coming. I invited John and Bri. They're coming later."

"Cal, Dude, Pluto welcome, and make yourselves at home."

Dude lifted Pluto so I could see what appeared on the front of the homemade T shirt around his body. On the front of it was an orange peace symbol. "Know this not be costume party. Pluto and me going to Loggerhead's Dog Costume Contest after boogie from here. Okay he wear here?"

I assured him the no costume rule only applied to people before Cal, Dude, and Pluto made a beeline for the kitchen and Charles said, "I called Burl, but he said you'd already invited him, and that he was bringing Shannon and the kids.

That's when I thought of John and Bri. Think it'd be good if they met each other."

"Not sure I follow, but they're more than welcome."

"Bri's interested in Wiccan and the Stones need to meet people who are interested but won't judge," Charles smiled. "Besides, we can't have a Halloween party with just witches. We need to have ghosts or at least ghost hunters."

Everyone appeared to be enjoying each other's company and especially the food. Cal had moved a chair to the side of the room and was singing; Barb was being a much better hostess than I was a host, when a knock at the door got my attention. Burl was on the porch and John and Bri were walking through the yard behind him.

I said, "Come in and join the party."

"Thank you, Brother Chris. Shannon and the kids are on their way. I must've driven faster."

Charles pushed past me, shook Burl's hand, and said, "Preacher, guess that means your car is faster than a broom. Nice to know."

Burl un-preacherlike rolled his eyes.

John and Bri were next to the door. "Chris, hope it's alright that Bri and I came. I tried to tell Charles you might not have wanted the entire population of the county at your house."

"John, Bri, the longer you know Charles, you'll learn it's impossible to convince him of anything. I'm glad he invited you. Come in."

Introductions were made and I went to the kitchen to get drinks for John and Bri. Between Cal's playing and the conversation, I must've missed the knock on the door.

Dude opened the door, took a quick step back, and said, "Chrisster, monster at door!"

I saw Lugh looking around the room like he was wondering which person would be the best choice for dinner. Shannon was standing next to him in an emerald green dress that looked as if it was from another era. Both kids were behind her. I crossed the room to greet the latest arrivals and to save Dude from the monster.

I said, "Welcome, please come in."

Shannon put her hand on my arm and squeezed as she said, "Thank you for inviting us. We needed to be with, umm, friends and the living."

I smiled and patted her hand. "Today must've been difficult."

Charles magically appeared beside me, bent to put his arms around Lugh's neck. "Lugh, my big baby, Happy Halloween. Want to go out back and stretch your legs? I bet Uncle Charles can find you a snack."

I said, "You have to forgive Charles. People are an afterthought when dogs are around."

Shannon unhooked Lugh's leash and said, "Chris, I understand."

On Charles and Lugh's way out back, Charles invited everyone to join them. The temperature was pleasant, and the house was growing smaller by the minute, so it was a good idea. Everyone followed except the Stones and Burl.

Roisin squeezed past her mom and wrapped her arms around my waist. "Thank you so much, Mr. Chris, I knew you'd find Dad's killer."

"Roisin, I was lucky. If it weren't for your brother and Lugh I wouldn't be here." I glanced at Desmond who smiled. I could be wrong, but it appeared sincere.

Shannon cleared her throat, "Desmond told me all

about yesterday. We are grateful to you and Charles for what you have done for us."

Burl walked over and hugged her. "Shannon, how are you? Today must be exceedingly hard on the whole family?"

Roisin moved beside her mother and grabbed Burls hand. "Mr. Burl, it was nice. We spread Dad's ashes in the flower garden. We were going to share them with the ocean but this way he's close to home."

Shannon followed Burl and Roisin to the back yard, leaving me alone in the house with the not so scary Desmond. I asked how he was.

He looked towards the back door and said, "Mom and little sis need me to be strong and help the family."

"You also need them, Desmond. Things will get better as long as the three of you stay close."

"Mr. Landrum, I'm going to take your advice and give people a chance to see who I am."

I put my hand on his shoulder. "If you need anything or just want to talk, you know how to find me."

"Thanks," he said then laughed. "Bet you never thought you'd be friends with a witch."

Dude stuck his head in the door, spotted Desmond and me, and said, "Yo, Sand, join us under the moon."

Desmond said, "On my way."

I looked at the young man and said, "Sand?"

Desmond smiled. "Yeah. First time I met Dude, we were on the beach. He called me Sand Witch."

"Oh," I said articulately.

"It's okay. He's a cool old guy," Desmond patted my arm before heading outside.

He was right. I never thought I'd be friends with a witch

or a witch family but there are lots of things I never thought. I headed out to join my ever growing party crowd. Lugh and Pluto were getting to know each other. Dude, Charles, and John, plus the addition of Desmond, supervised the meeting, probably to keep Lugh from devouring Pluto in one bite. Off to the side, Cal was playing his guitar with Burl, Roisin, and Barb listening nearby. Across the yard, Bri was standing by herself and watching the activities.

I made my way across the yard to Shannon and motioned her to follow as I made my way to Bri.

"Bri, I'd like you to meet Shannon Stone. Shannon, this is Bri Rice."

They smiled and shook hands.

Shannon nodded at Bri and said, "I believe you were at my husband's funeral ritual the other day. Am I correct?"

Bri looked as if she wanted to vanish. "Umm, yes. I'm so sorry. I didn't mean to intrude. I was curious."

"Mrs. Rice, it is okay. You were not there to harm but with a true interest. How could I fault you for that?" Shannon's hand went to Bri's shoulder.

"Please call me Bri. Thank you for understanding."

"Bri, call me Shannon, if you have questions, please ask. My kids and I welcome sincere discussions. Chris can vouch for that."

I smiled and said, "Bri, you need to watch Roisin. She's smarter than the rest of us and according to her brother, she's a very old soul."

Shannon said, "You are correct. My little nymph is wise beyond her years." She motioned in the direction of the rest of the party. "I believe it's safe if you leave Bri and me to share a conversation."

I took the hint. When I looked back, the women were

sitting on the ground talking like they had known each other for centuries. I made it halfway back to Barb when I saw Cindy standing in the side yard.

"Chief, did someone call in a noise complaint about Cal's singing?"

"An invitation certainly didn't bring me here. Suppose mine was lost in the mail or the owl dropped it."

"Owl?"

"You're not a Harry Potter fan. Anyway, not important."

"I would love it if you and Larry could stop by. This wasn't really a planned thing."

I wondered if it was a crime to not invite the Chief to the party she just crashed.

She smiled. "Messing with you. I finished at the office and wanted to talk to you on my way home. Larry and I always go out to dinner and a costume party in Charleston on Halloween."

"Didn't know you were into that sort of thing."

"You could write a novel on what you don't know about me. I'll leave it at that. The reason I'm here is a preemptive strike on you calling about Dr. Robinson and his wife."

"What's happened?"

"Dr. Robinson has been arrested for selling drugs and involuntary manslaughter with more charges pending further investigation."

"More charges?"

"The investigation just started. I'm not positive about Georgia law, but I've heard of a case where a drug dealer was charged with felony murder when one of his customers died of an overdose. Dr. Robinson is out of my jurisdiction. I only need to help the Sheriff with his case against Erica, the shrill unstable double murderer. That's enough."

"Chief ,thanks for letting me know. Sure you can't stay?"

"Nope, need to get my zombie on and cruise on to Charleston." Cindy turned and headed to her pickup truck.

I watched Cindy go only to hear her yell back, "Hey, old geezer, think you can wait until after Thanksgiving to find another body?"

Charles appeared at my side and said, "Got a question. Before Desmond left yesterday, why'd you ask him if the door to the haunted house was open when he and Lugh saved us?"

"I would've sworn I heard it close before I saw Erika. Must've been mistaken."

Charles slowly nodded. "Or a ghost opened it so Desmond and Lugh could save us."

I waited for him to laugh at his joke. It never came.

"Charles, I'm sticking with being mistaken."

He put his arm around my shoulder. "If you say so."

"Let's head back to the party and be thankful for our new and old friends."

Cal was singing "Monster Mash," country style at the top of his lungs, the atmosphere was becoming more festive, and the horrific experiences of the last month were disappearing just as the sea fog had.

BILL NOEL'S FOLLY BEACH

SOUTH CAROLINA

Charleston
East Second St
Huron Ave
Center Street
Erie Ave
Indian Ave
Chris's House
Sandbar Lane
West Second St
Hudson Ave
Charles's Apartment
First Light
Cooper Ave
Ashley Ave
Arctic Ave
Boneyard Beach
Morris Island Lighthouse
Marsh
Folly River
Washout
Pier
Folly Beach County Park

1 Rita's
2 Dude's surf shop *
3 Sand Dollar
4 Haunted House *
5 Loggerhead's
6 Snapper Jacks
7 St. James Gate
8 Surf Bar
9 Cal's *
10 Mr. John's Beach Store
11 Landrum Gallery/Barb's Books *
12 The Crab Shack
13 City Hall/Public Safety
14 Sean Aker, Attorney *
15 Planet Follywood
16 Woody's Pizza
17 The Washout
18 Post Office
19 Pewter Hardware *
20 Lost Dog Cafe
21 Bert's Market
22 The Edge *

* From my imagination to yours.

About the Authors

Bill Noel is the bestselling author of nineteen novels in the popular Folly Beach Mystery series. The award-winning novelist is also a fine arts photographer and lives in Louisville, Kentucky, with his wife, Susan, and his off kilter imagination.

Angelica Cruz counts Halloween among her favorite days of the year so what better setting for her debut novel. Ms. Cruz lives near Elizabethtown, Kentucky, with her husband Hector, two dogs, a bird, two cats, and four chickens.

Learn more about the series and the author by visiting www.billnoel.com.

Made in the USA
Columbia, SC
18 August 2021

43850624R00159